"El!" he yelled. "What is going on?"

She froze. Looked up at the man. It was Jake.

Ella grabbed hold of him, then turned to see if her attacker was still in the stairwell. He was gone.

Pull yourself together. Now!

"I—I just got turned around in the lot," she said, straightening her dress. "Then the elevator malfunctioned, and I had to take the stairs back down."

"Are you okay?"

"Yeah," Ella lied. "I'm fine."

Jake kept an arm wrapped firmly around her shoulders on the way back to the casino. "I've got to catch you up on what happened."

"Can't wait to hear all about it," Ella mumbled, wondering when she'd get up the nerve to tell Jake the truth.

HOMICIDE AT VINCENT VINEYARD

———

DENISE N. WHEATLEY

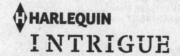

To my little besties, Nina and Brooke Heintzelman. Thank you for
helping me plot out this book. Also, please do not tell your parents
about this…

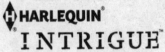

HARLEQUIN®
INTRIGUE™

Recycling programs
for this product may
not exist in your area.

ISBN-13: 978-1-335-59059-6

Homicide at Vincent Vineyard

Harlequin Enterprises ULC
22 Adelaide St. West, 41st Floor
Toronto, Ontario M5H 4E3, Canada
www.Harlequin.com

Printed in U.S.A.

Denise N. Wheatley loves happy endings and the art of storytelling. Her novels run the romance gamut, and she strives to pen entertaining books that embody matters of the heart. She's an RWA member and holds a BA in English from the University of Illinois. When Denise isn't writing, she enjoys watching true-crime TV and chatting with readers. Follow her on social media.

Instagram: @Denise_Wheatley_Writer
Twitter: @DeniseWheatley
BookBub: @DeniseNWheatley
Goodreads: Denise N. Wheatley

Books by Denise N. Wheatley

Harlequin Intrigue

A West Coast Crime Story

The Heart-Shaped Murders
Danger in the Nevada Desert
Homicide at Vincent Vineyard

Cold Case True Crime
Bayou Christmas Disappearance
Backcountry Cover-Up

Visit the Author Profile page at Harlequin.com.

CAST OF CHARACTERS

Jake Love—The new chief of police in Clemmington, California.

Ella Bowman—Jake's girlfriend and survivor of the Numeric Serial Killer.

Don Vincent—Murder victim who owned Vincent Vineyard prior to his death.

Claire Vincent—Don's wife and COO of Vincent Vineyard.

Tyler Vincent—Don's oldest son and co–vice president of Vincent Vineyard.

Greer Vincent—Don's youngest son and co–vice president of Vincent Vineyard.

Manuel Ruiz—Manager of Vincent Vineyard.

Jada Vincent—Tyler's wife and sales director of Vincent Vineyard.

Faith Vincent—Greer's wife and sales representative at Vincent Vineyard.

Chapter One

"You're late," Ella murmured into her cell phone.

She eyed the entrance of Clemmington, California's fall harvest festival, making sure Jake wasn't walking through the iron arbor as she spoke. A group of rowdy teenagers appeared, leaping in the air to see who could reach the maple leaf vines hanging from the ten-foot-tall archway first. But there was no sign of Jake.

"I'll be leaving the station soon!" he yelled so loudly that Ella pulled the phone away from her ear. "I promise!"

She chuckled at his enthusiasm. While their relationship was still fairly new, Ella felt as though she'd known him for years. They had grown close after Jake's brother, Miles, and her sister, Charlotte, apprehended Nevada's Numeric Serial Killer—the man who also happened to be Ella's ex-boyfriend. It had taken Ella some time to recuperate from the ordeal. Soon after the arrest, she submitted a leave of absence from her job as a traveling nurse, left River Valley behind and moved to Clemmington temporarily to be closer to Jake and Charlotte.

"You know," he continued, "considering I'm Clemmington's newly appointed chief of police, you're lucky I even have time to attend the festival."

"*Extremely* lucky. Your dedication to the force is awe-inspiring. But I think even the former chief would approve of you taking a break every now and then," Ella said, referring to his father, Kennedy, who'd retired from the position before recommending that his eldest son take over.

"I know he would. And I'm only kidding. *I'm* the lucky one. I hope you know how happy I am that you're here with me."

"And I'm happy to be here," Ella purred, her golden-brown cheeks tingling from the warmth of his words. "Spending time with you, Charlotte and the baby has really helped me get through everything. Your whole family has, really."

"Well, just know that the Loves are always here for you."

"Thanks, babe."

A gust of wind blew Ella's long dark hair across her face. She pulled a few loose waves behind her ears and pushed through the crowd, observing long lines of festivalgoers wrapped around bucket-toss, Skee-Ball and duck-pond game booths. Laughter mixed with screams flew overhead as colorful amusement rides twirled in the air. The scents of freshly popped popcorn and hot apple cider mingled with beef chili and funnel cake. But the mouthwatering smell of french fries sent Ella's stomach rumbling.

"Uh-oh," she uttered as the delicious aroma rerouted her black combat boots in the direction of the food stalls. "All these yummy eats they're serving have me in a trance. I see Pauline's Potato Pit Stop up ahead, and I haven't eaten since breakfast. I was trying to hold out and wait for you to get here. But I am starving, and these potatoes are calling my name."

"Please don't wait for me. Go ahead. Enjoy yourself. Eat, play a few games and make sure you stop by Sofia's Homemade Wine stand. She does a curated flight sampler that you have got to try. It contains a little bit of everything. Sparking, white, red, sweet… You'll love it. It's pricey, but worth it. I'll text you as soon as I'm on my way. I shouldn't be much longer."

"Okay, babe. See you soon."

Ella approached Pauline's, debating what to get. From smoked and loaded baked potatoes to sweet potato waffle fries and garlic mashed potatoes, the choices ran the gamut. She settled on an order of cheesy taco fries, then set out to explore the rest of the event.

"Hey, El!"

Pivoting in the direction of the familiar voice, Ella spotted Officer Underwood, who was standing in line at the Ferris wheel. "Hey, how are you?"

"Great! Where's Chief Regé-Jean Page?" he joked, referring to Jake's uncanny resemblance to the *Bridgerton* star.

"He's still down at the station. But he'll be here soon."

"That man is such a workaholic. Hopefully I'll see you two before we leave."

"Sounds good. Have fun!"

As Ella continued along the festival trail, the air began to cool. She zipped her beige leather jacket and glanced up at the deep purple sky. Dusk had already descended upon the vast grounds. Dark clouds billowed across the setting sun, marking an eerie desolation on several festival attractions.

The petting zoo pen sat empty as the goats, sheep, ponies and alpacas had already been hauled away. Children had abandoned the wooden crates stacked with pumpkin varieties. Fortune tellers packed up their tarot cards and crystal balls, leaving their bejeweled velvet tents behind. The tractor-pulled wagon carrying attendees on a tour of the scenic orchard sat empty, having unloaded its last group for the evening.

I hope they all made it back safely, Ella thought, remembering how Jake once told her that fifteen thousand people disappear from festival hayride wagons each year.

"Hello, young lady," someone croaked behind her.

Ella jumped, turning toward the creepy voice. A tall slender man swung his lanky arm to the side and smiled, revealing a row of jagged gray teeth. "How would you like to try your luck at making it out of Abel's Amazing Corn Maze alive?"

Her wide-set amber eyes narrowed at the sight of his spotty pale skin and gaunt cheeks. Strands of long white hair stuck out from underneath his distressed straw hat. His frail frame barely held his dingy overalls in place. A sign above him read Wander Your Way Through To The End. Or Die Trying... It was a scene straight out of a horror movie.

"I—I think I'll pass," Ella stammered, backing away from the maze.

"Oh, come on," he grunted, taking a step toward her. "What have you got to lose? This is the easiest maze in all of California. Even children have made their way out, all alone."

No sooner than the words had escaped his

hollow mouth, a group of kids came running over. They shoved their tickets inside his skeletal hand, then darted inside.

"Those little ones are my regulars," he said. "This is their third time through the maze today. Oh, and one thing I forgot to mention. If you do make it to the other side, there's a prize. Depending on your preference, you'll receive either a free hot chocolate from Beatrice's Bakery, or a glass of wine from Sofia's Winery. Your choice."

Ella could hear the children who'd entered the corn maze laughing hysterically.

Now you have been known to conquer a maze or two during your festival days back in River Valley.

She glanced at her watch, remembering that she also had time to kill while waiting on Jake to arrive.

"*Well*, why not," Ella said before taking a quick bite of fries, then shoving the bag inside her tote. "I could certainly go for a glass of Zinfandel from Sofia's."

"Ahh, yes. Now that's what I like to hear. Admission for adults is ten dollars. But for you, my dear, it's free. Don't fall into a daze as you walk through the maze, and I'll see you on the other side. I hope…"

Ella side-eyed the strange man. "You're good,

you know that? You almost had me scared to walk through this thing. *Almost...*"

He gave her a slow wink that sent chills up her back. "The only thing to fear is fear itself. Isn't that what Franklin D. Roosevelt once said? Good luck, ma'am."

She quickly slipped past the man and entered the maze, ignoring pangs of uneasiness banging around inside her chest. Playing it safe with a game of Whac-A-Mole or even axe-throwing would've been just fine. But she'd never been one to turn down a challenge. Or a free glass of wine.

The moment Ella hit the dirt path, darkness descended upon her. She'd underestimated the height of the cornstalk hovering overhead. Dried leaves blew against her body, slicing at the exposed skin on her face and hands. She pulled out her cell and turned on the flashlight, shining it along the rugged trail.

"What have I gotten myself into?" she muttered, picking up speed as she reached the end of the aisle.

Boom!

Ella ducked down, almost falling to the ground. Slow to stand, she noticed a zombie scarecrow looming up above. She'd almost knocked over the frightening figure, unable to see its deathly gray makeup and shredded black clothing through the darkness. A faux black crow was perched on a wooden beam, squawking loudly as its red eyes glowed in the dark.

Abel didn't mention this maze being haunted...

Ella scrambled to her feet, suddenly anxious to find the exit. She made a right turn and held her phone in the air, searching for the signs. There were none.

What the...

She jogged to the end of the pathway, then made a quick left, her thick soles skidding across mounds of straw-covered dirt. Within seconds, she reached the corner of that aisle. It was a dead end.

"Dammit!"

Ella spun around and rushed down the long trail, heaving as panic began to tighten her airways. The four-way intersection revealed no signs, and no clues leading to the exit.

Stop. Stay calm. Listen for the voices.

She stood still, waiting to hear the screams and laughter of fellow mazegoers. There were none.

"Just keep going," she muttered, her mind spinning with confusion.

Ella ran full speed ahead, ignoring the clouds of dust kicking up around her and cornstalks slashing against her body.

"Wrong way!" someone yelled.

She fell against a massive object, then dropped to the ground.

"*Ouch*," Ella uttered, grabbing her lower back. She looked up. A spell of dizziness blurred her vision. Within seconds, she was able to make out a heavyset man dressed in a tattered plaid shirt, creeping along the edge of the cornstalks.

"Well hot damn!" he yelled. "That must've hurt." He cackled loudly, then reached for her.

"Get the hell away from me!" she screamed.

"Hey! This is *my* turf, lady. And if I see you again, I can guarantee you won't make it outta here alive. Cuz Abel sure ain't coming to save ya!"

He let out a piercing howl, then ran off. The second he was out of her sight, Ella hopped up and ran in the opposite direction. She grabbed her cell phone and pounded the side button.

"Siri, call Jake!"

"Calling Jake."

It went straight to voice mail.

She disconnected the call and slowed down, gathering her bearings.

Take it easy. Deep breaths. This is an amusement attraction, for God's sake. Just keep going until you find your way out...

Ella moved forward. Another dead end appeared up ahead. This time, she didn't freak out.

She simply stopped, slumped down onto a bale of hay and tried Jake again.

"You have reached the voice mail box of Chief Jake Love—"

She hung up.

Why would you let that creepy man talk you into this mess? Ella asked herself, realizing that no glass of wine was worth this type of trauma. *Now you're gonna end up on the five o'clock news—another fall festival victim, gone missing...*

Dialing 9-1-1 crossed her mind. But she couldn't bring herself to do it. If those kids could find their way out of the maze, so could she.

Come on. Suck it up. Get on your feet and find your way out of here.

Ella stood, pulling in a mass of cool air. Just as she set off toward the end of the aisle, something sharp poked her in the back.

"*Ow!*" she yelled, swinging her arm in the air. "Look, man, this is not funny!"

She spun a three-sixty turn, expecting the heavyset zombie farmer to pop out from the behind the cornstalks. He didn't. No one did.

"I am not amused, you…you *clown.* Come on out! Show your face."

Silence.

Maybe it was just a cornstalk blowing in the wind.

"Keep moving," Ella told herself right before

someone grabbed her jacket and knocked her to the ground.

"That is *it*!" she screamed. "Abel! Come and get me the hell out of here!"

Ella pressed her palms against the trail, struggling to stand. Pellets of dried dirt and splintered stalks tore into her skin. She didn't care. Escaping the maze was all that mattered.

The moment she rolled over onto her knees, a figure dressed in all black emerged from the stalks.

No, no, no!

"Somebody help me!" Ella screamed.

"Miss!" a voice called out in the distance. "Where are you!"

"I'm over he—"

The figure swooped in and covered her mouth with a gloved hand. "Shut up!" he rasped, putting her in a headlock and dragging her into the cornstalks.

"No! Let me go!" Ella kicked her legs wildly, attempting to scream. But her mouth was still covered, and her throat was jammed in the crook of the assailant's arm.

"Who are you?" she wheezed. "Why are you doing this to me?"

He remained silent, yanking her body into the stalks. Despite ripping at his arm, the pressure didn't let up. Ella dug her heels into the dirt. Her calves burned as the traction inched her back toward the trail.

Keep fighting. Keep fighting!

Beams of light shined down the aisle.

"Ma'am!" someone called out as footsteps pounded in her direction.

"*Lucky bitch*," the attacker barked in Ella's ear before tossing her off to the side and vanishing into the stalks.

A festival security guard ran over. "Are you okay?"

She gasped, clutching her neck while rolling over. "No, I've been attacked!"

"*Attacked*?" he shouted while helping Ella to her feet. "By who?"

"I have no idea. At first I thought it was one of the carnival workers, playing a joke on me. But it wasn't. This person didn't have on a costume. He was dressed in all black and trying to hurt me."

"Did you see which way he went?"

"That way," she heaved, pointing toward the cornstalks.

Security stared into what appeared to be the dark abyss, his twisted expression weary. "It was probably some kid, pulling a silly prank. I'm sure he's long gone by now. Why don't we get you out of here and call the authorities?"

Ella didn't bother to tell him that she was dating the chief of police. Her only focus was getting to safety.

Maybe he's right. Could've just been a kid playing a prank...

Her phone buzzed.

Jake, finally!

She eyed the screen, desperate to tell him what just happened. But it wasn't Jake. It was a text message sent from an anonymous number.

Ella's heart pounded inside her throat as she swiped open the message.

You may have made it out of the corn maze, but you won't make it out of Clemmington alive. Watch your back. Because I know what you did...

Chapter Two

Jake sat calmly despite shards of anger tearing through his veins. He glared at the man authorities suspected had attacked Ella at the festival.

Deep breaths, he thought, clenching his jaw while his knees bounced against the edge of the table.

The stench of wet paint stung Jake's nostrils as renovations to the Clemmington police station dragged on. Their new state-of-the-art forensics lab had sparked his father's desire to spruce up the entire building right before his retirement. What was meant to be a farewell gift to his team resulted in a huge pain as all the dust, electrical cords, power tools and construction crew members took over their workspace.

"So," Jake began, his tightened lips barely parting, "you *are* admitting that you were at the festival on the evening of the fifteenth?"

"Yeah," the young man mumbled. "I was there. But I didn't attack anybody."

"But you were running through the corn maze, harassing the attendees. Is that correct?"

The short husky suspect leaned back in his chair, balancing himself on its rear legs. He glared at Jake through lowered eyes, his baby face contorting into a menacing snarl.

"Please answer the question, Mr. Montero," Miles chimed in, who'd insisted on participating in the interrogation alongside his big brother.

"I know how much Ella means to you, man," Miles had told Jake right before he entered the room. "You're the chief of police now. All eyes are on you, and there's no room for error. I just wanna be there to make sure everything goes smoothly."

"All right, all right. Fine," Jake had finally agreed.

And now, almost two hours later, the brothers had yet to pull a confession out of their suspect.

"We have eyewitnesses stating that they saw you tearing through those cornstalks," Jake pressed.

"They may have seen *somebody*, but they didn't see me."

Through the corners of his eyes, Jake glanced over at the reflective glass window. Ella and Charlotte were standing on the other side of it. He hated the idea of them watching him fail. Ella had been through enough, having been attacked by her serial killer ex-boyfriend shortly before he was apprehended. This assault could've been enough to send her over the edge. But she was tough and hadn't allowed a prank at a small-town festival to break her.

"We're not getting anywhere with this one," Miles muttered in Jake's ear.

"Yeah, but I'm not ready to give up just yet."

Jake slid his chair closer to the suspect's. "Mr. Montero, you do know that there are security cameras all around the festival grounds, don't you?"

The suspect's snarl morphed into a look of surprise. He stared down at his hands, picking at his dirty fingernails. "No. I didn't."

"Well, there are. So whatever you did, we'll see it. We're just waiting on the surveillance footage."

"Not only that," Miles interjected, "but those eyewitnesses we mentioned will be giving official statements, along with the security guards who were on the premises that night. We'll be doing a lineup as well. So here's your chance, Mr. Montero. Whatever you're not telling us, we're gonna find out. Let us hear it from you first. What was your reasoning behind the—"

The suspect leaned forward and pounded his fist against the steel table. "I'm done trying to convince you all that I'm innocent. I refuse to answer another question. I wanna talk to a lawyer. Now!"

Jake slumped down in his chair. Just as he grabbed his file, there was knock at the door.

"Why don't you get that while I keep an eye on Mr. Montero?" Miles told him.

"What do you mean *keep an eye on me*? I'm not under arrest, am I? I can leave anytime I want, can't I? That's what your boy told me when I first walked in here."

"My *boy*? His name is Chief Love. Show some respect, young man."

Ignoring the suspect, Jake lumbered toward the door on legs that had numbed after sitting for so long. Charlotte was standing on the other side.

"Hey," she whispered. "Can I talk to you for a sec?"

"Of course."

He stepped out and closed the door behind him, flinching at the sight of her weary red eyes. Her downturned lips told him that she wasn't here to deliver good news.

"What's going on?" he asked.

"It's Ella. She said the guy you're interrogating isn't the person who attacked her."

"She did? But it was so dark out there. I thought she didn't get a good look at him."

"She didn't. However, judging by the quick

glances that she did get, Ella doesn't remember her attacker being as stocky as this guy."

Jake dropped his head in his hand. "Is she sure? Because we've got witnesses who saw him running through the corn maze, harassing patrons."

"She's sure. The man you're interrogating is shorter and much bulkier than her assailant."

"All right." He sighed, his arms falling by his sides. "Good to know, especially since this guy just lawyered up. Back to the drawing board."

"Have the festival organizers sent over the surveillance footage?"

"Not yet."

"Well, when they do, I'd be more than happy to review it with you, Miles and Ella. Even though I'm technically on a work hiatus from River Valley PD, I can't just shake my sergeant duties. I'm all in on this. I cannot have my sister out here randomly being attacked. Not after everything she's been through."

"I agree. I'm hoping this is all a result of some stupid joke being played by a teenager. I'd heard there were groups of unruly high schoolers acting out during the entire festival. *Dammit*, I should've been there with her. Then this never would've happened in the first place."

"Come on," Charlotte said, giving his arm a reassuring pat. "Don't do that. This isn't your fault. Who would've thought that some goofball would be running around the festival, harassing attendees? Ella understands that you've taken on a big job and can't be by her side twenty-four seven. Chalk this one up as a fluke and let it go. Your team will do their job of catching whoever did it. In the meantime, let's just make sure our girl is okay."

Jake stood straight up and squared his shoulders. "You're right. I just want Ella to know that we're taking her attack seriously. But for now, I'll send Mr. Montero home."

"And I'll get back to Ella. Trust me, she knows you're taking this seriously. She also knows that investigations take time, and most cases don't get solved overnight."

"But does she feel safe?" he asked as they headed down the hallway. "Ella came to Clemmington looking for security. And peace. *I'm* the one who's supposed to give her those things."

"We all are, Jake. And we will. Let's just make an effort to keep a closer eye on her."

The pair entered the observation room. Jake went straight to Ella, wrapping his arms around her. "Hey, how are you holding up?"

"Okay, I guess. I didn't think I'd be back inside a police station this soon. But yet, here I am."

His chest pulled when her body stiffened

against his. "I'm so sorry, El. Charlotte told me you don't think this guy is our suspect. But we've got a plan. That surveillance footage from the festival will give us some answers. We'll get the official statements on record from the eyewitnesses and security team. And I'll send my guys out to patrol the streets. You never know. Maybe our perp will get himself into more trouble and we'll apprehend him that way."

"Let's hope so. Like you've been saying, maybe this was all just a silly teenage prank."

He planted a soft kiss on her forehead. "On the bright side, I've got some exciting news to share with you and my family tonight during dinner. Something I've been thinking about ever since I took over as chief of police."

"I could use some good news."

Charlotte gave Ella's hand a squeeze. "Why don't we go back to my place until Jake gets off work?"

"Better yet," Jake interjected, glancing at his watch, "why don't you two meet us at my parents' house later tonight? I don't think Miles and I are getting out of here any time soon. Is that okay with you?" he asked Ella.

"Of course," she murmured, her head falling against his chest.

"Come on. Let's get you out of here."

Jake led her toward the exit, hoping the incident at the festival boiled down to teenage antics and nothing more sinister…

"HOW ARE YOU DOING, SWEETHEART?" Betty asked Ella. The matriarch of the Love family had been fussing over her ever since she'd arrived at the house.

"She's fine, Mom," Jake told her, sensing Ella's discomfort at being the center of attention as she shifted in her seat. "Why don't you have a seat and enjoy this delicious meal you prepared?"

"Yes, honey," her husband, Kennedy, chimed in. "The food is getting cold."

Lena, Jake's sister, pulled out Betty's chair. "You sit down, and I'll make your plate. You've done enough."

"Ugh." Her mother sighed, plopping down into the chair. "Fine, but not too much food now. I'm trying to watch my weight."

Ignoring Betty's request, Lena piled a rib eye steak, lobster tail, roasted corn on the cob and grilled asparagus onto a dish.

"This girl doesn't listen," Betty muttered in her husband's direction.

"So, Mom," Miles said in between bites of a crescent roll, "to what do we owe this fabulous dinner?"

"Well," she began, tapping Lena's hand in an

attempt to stop her hefty pour of Cabernet Sauvignon, "your brother said he's got some good news that he'd like to share with the family tonight. I figured what better way to celebrate than with a nice surf and turf and homemade apple cobbler."

"Homemade apple cobbler? *Mmm*," Jake repeated, relishing in the warmth that illuminated throughout the Love family's home. The mood was festive, with Ella even appearing more relaxed as she settled against the back of her chair and gave him a wink.

"All right, son," Kennedy said. "Let's hear it. What's this big news you've been so eager to share?"

After taking a long sip of wine, Jake cleared his throat.

"Remember Don Vincent, the owner of Vincent Vineyard who was murdered last year?"

Kennedy set down his fork. "Of course I remember. How could I forget? Don was a great man. A well-respected pillar of the Clemmington community. His charity efforts helped send underprivileged kids to college, put food on tables, provided gifts for families during the holidays—" He paused, his words catching in his throat.

"It's okay, honey," Betty said, clutching his hand.

"No. It isn't. My one regret in life will always

be that I never solved his murder." Kennedy's weary gaze shifted toward Jake. "I'm sorry, son. Please, continue. What about Don?"

"Well, now that I've taken over as chief of police, I'm going to reopen Don's cold case. See if we can get it solved."

Taking a breath, Kennedy pressed his hands together. "*Jake*. I... I don't even know what to say. Except, *wow*. I wasn't expecting that. It would be wonderful for the Vincent family and the entire Clemmington community if you could solve Don's murder. But let me be the first to warn you. It's gonna be tough. We covered a lot of ground during the initial investigation. Where would you even start?"

"The best place would be with your old files. You compiled a ton of information and leads. Persons of interest, surveillance footage from the vineyard, interviews with employees and family members. I'm even planning to pull the evidence that was collected at the crime scene and have it reexamined."

"I like that idea," Lena interjected, who'd moved back to Clemmington after working for the LAPD and now served as the head of Forensics. "Since we have the new lab, I can retest the evidence and see if anything comes up that wasn't discovered during the first go-round."

Kennedy's grin widened. "I am loving this

plan of action. It would mean the world to me if we finally captured Don's killer."

"I'm sorry," Betty said, pointing in her husband's direction, "but did I just hear you say *we*?"

He shrugged, glancing around the table as wrinkles of confusion creased his forehead. "Yes. Why?"

"I'm just wondering who exactly is included in this *we*. Because last time I checked, you no longer work for the Clemmington PD. So there will be no *we* when it comes to solving this case. Leave that up to our new chief of police and the rest of the force. You'll be too busy vacationing and taking care of our grandbaby to work on the investigation anyway."

A hushed silence swept through the room. It was disrupted when Kennedy snickered quietly.

"Welp, the lady of the house has spoken. Nevertheless, Jake, I trust that you and the rest of the team will get the case solved. If you need any assistance or advice though, you know where to find me—"

Betty threw him a look that stopped Kennedy mid-sentence. He waved his white linen napkin in the air, declaring defeat.

"Thanks, Dad," Jake said. He turned to David Hudson, a detective with the Clemmington PD and Lena's boyfriend. "What do you think of all this, Dave? You were a big part of the first investigation. Who do you think should be questioned first?"

"I'd say start with Don's wife, Claire. I remember her being a main suspect when the murder first occurred."

"What would've given you *that* impression?" Miles quipped through a sarcastic smirk. "The fact that she was having an affair with Alan Monroe, or that she was draining Don's bank account without putting much work in at the vineyard?"

"C. All the above."

"Wait, who is Alan Monroe?" Charlotte asked. "I am so curious about this case now. Ella, why do I get the feeling you and I are gonna insert ourselves in this investigation to help solve it?"

When Ella remained silent, Jake gave her a playful nudge. "I'd actually love it if you chimed in on this case, babe."

"Mmm-hmm," she muttered while pushing a forkful of asparagus across her plate.

Blaming her dry reaction on the rough day she'd had, Jake propped his arm against the back of her chair and leaned in Charlotte's direction. "To answer your question, Alan is the owner of Creekside Winery."

"Also known as Vincent's Vineyard's main competition," Miles pointed out.

"Exactly. It's located a couple of towns over, and word on the street is that Alan began having an affair with Don's wife, Claire, a few years ago after they'd met at a wine convention in San Francisco."

"Ooh, that would be pretty scandalous if it's true." Charlotte tapped Ella. "Are you getting all this?"

She replied with a slight nod, her eyes remaining fixated on her plate.

"Hey," Jake whispered in Ella's ear, "are you okay?"

"Yeah…just feeling a little headachy all of a sudden."

Miles held his hand in the air. "Hold on, now. We can't just focus on Claire as our main suspect. What about her two sons, Tyler and Greer?"

A loud gag startled everyone at the table. They turned to Ella, who was gulping down mouthfuls of water.

Jake jumped to his feet and slapped her back. "Are you all right?"

"I—fi… I'm fine! A piece of asparagus must've gotten caught in my throat."

"But you weren't eating any—" Jake stopped abruptly when she threw him a death stare.

Something was definitely off. Was it the attack at the festival? Had it triggered thoughts of being assaulted by her ex? Or was it something deeper?

"Please," Ella said to Miles, "continue with what you were saying."

"I was just asking about Tyler and Greer, who took over the vineyard after their father was killed. Rumor has it they may have been behind his murder."

"I always thought one of them had something to do with it," Kennedy said. "Especially that older one, Tyler."

"Same here," Jake interjected. "He and I went to high school together, and even back then, I remember him being super flashy and arrogant. Once he graduated and worked his way up to vice president of the vineyard, his ego inflated to the point of combustion."

"That it did," Kennedy agreed. "And during the time that I was investigating Don's death, it came out that both sons were at odds with their father. Especially Tyler."

"Why were they at odds?" Charlotte asked. "Were the sons trying to take over the vineyard?"

"Something like that," Jake told her. "Tyler and Greer both serve as vice presidents. But neither of them had the best relationship with Don. The business had begun to tear them apart because the sons wanted to take Vincent Vineyard to the next level. Their goal was to keep up with the current trends and give Creekside Winery a run for its money."

"And let me guess," Lena said. "Don was resistant to that idea."

"Very much so," Kennedy replied. "After investigating the case, I felt like a vineyard expert. I learned all about how the sons wanted to expand the planted grape varieties and incorporate newer technologies, digital trends and winemaking equipment. They were also pushing their father to build a visitor area for tastings and group tours. But Don refused. He'd insisted that his old-school way was the only way. He had achieved success by producing a smaller output of wine while growing limited grape varieties, and felt that his simple, grassroots marketing efforts were bringing in a steady stream of business. So in his mind, he'd thought, why fix what isn't broken?"

"*Humph*," Betty huffed. "Poor man. His unwillingness to broaden the business may have very well cost him his life."

Kennedy polished off the rest of his stcak, then reclined in his chair. "We all had our suspicions of a few key family members. Employees too, for that matter. Too bad we couldn't put it all together and prove who'd done it. But I have no doubt that the new Chief Love will. Thank you for reopening this case, son."

"Of course. I'm definitely feeling confident. Especially now that we've got a secret weapon on the team that we didn't have last year."

"And by secret weapon," Lena said, leaning toward Jake, "are you referring to me?"

"I most certainly am." He held his glass in the air, tipping it in her direction. "Thank you. All of you. I appreciate your faith in me. Trust that I won't let you down."

"We've got all the faith in the world in you," Kennedy assured him.

"And on that note," Betty said as she began clearing the table, "why don't I bring out the apple cobbler, vanilla bean ice cream and coffee, then we switch the subject to something a little more pleasant?"

"I'd like that," Ella muttered, hopping up and gathering several dishes.

Jake's brows furrowed with concern. "Here, let me help you." He attempted to take a couple of the plates.

"I got it!" she snapped, jerking away and rushing toward the kitchen.

"Is she all right?" Miles asked.

Charlotte grabbed her plate and went after Ella. "I don't know, but I'll find out. Jake, just relax and finish your dinner."

He took a seat just as Betty reached across the table and patted his forearm. "She's probably still shaken up from the attack at the festival, honey. Not to mention that killer ex-boyfriend of hers."

"I agree," Kennedy added. "All that violence would have a negative effect on anybody. This talk of Don Vincent's murder probably got to her too. Just give her some time, son."

"I will." He peered at the doorway, debating whether he should check on Ella. When Lena grabbed the bottle of wine and refilled his glass, he decided against it.

"Speaking of the attack at the festival," she said, "have you identified a suspect yet?"

"No, unfortunately." Jake paused at the faint sound of Ella sobbing. It burned through his ear-drums, igniting a fire deep inside his gut. "But I will. Trust me, I will."

Chapter Three

Ella sat in the passenger seat of Jake's car, twisting the jade cocktail rings adorning her perfectly manicured hands. The pair were headed to an exclusive wine tasting event at Vincent Vineyard. She thought she'd seen the last of the place several years ago. Yet here she was, heading to the venue she'd grown to dread in hopes of gathering new intel before Jake officially reopened Don Vincent's murder investigation.

When Ella learned of Jake's plan during the family dinner, she almost fell from her chair. She'd thought her ties to the Vincent family had been severed for good.

Not so fast, the cruel universe whispered in her ear.

Ella's stomach flipped as Jake pulled into the vineyard's winding driveway. The breathtaking Tuscan-inspired winery, with its tan limestone exterior, terra-cotta rooftop and sprawling hillside greenery, exuded a charming old-world European style. When she'd first laid eyes on the sprawling establishment way back when, Ella had been captivated. But now, it brought on feelings of disgust.

"This place is amazing, isn't it?" Jake asked.

"It is," she replied, her low tone laced with reluctance.

Ella envisioned the Vincent family's reaction upon seeing her. Thoughts of them sent pangs of anxiety flipping through her stomach.

Stop it. You can do this.

Her eyes stung at the sight of the arched wooden doorway. A valet driver opened Ella's door and offered his hand. She paused, far from ready to exit the vehicle.

"You ready?" Jake asked, clearly confused by her hesitancy.

"Yep, I'm ready," she lied.

"Listen, I really appreciate you coming here with me tonight. But if you don't want to be a part of this investigation, you don't have to. I just know how much you enjoyed assisting Charlotte with her cases back in River Valley. Plus, since you're taking a break from nursing, I figured you'd want to occupy your time with something interesting."

"Absolutely. I'm happy to help in any way that I can."

She stiffened underneath Jake's curious stare.

It was as if he could sense her dishonesty. The urge to tell him what was bothering her lingered on the tip of Ella's tongue. But she swallowed it down. Now was not the time.

Jake held her close as the pair made their way up the curved stone staircase.

"I remember how tough it was for my sister when she took a break from the LAPD after being attacked," he said. "Lena moved back to Clemmington and got so bored sitting around my parents' house that she started investigating the Heart-Shaped Murders' case on her own. That almost got her killed."

"Well, I certainly won't be doing anything that dangerous to occupy my time. But again, I'm all in on assisting you."

"Good," Jake murmured, covering her lips with a lingering kiss. "I can't tell you how much that means to me."

"Oh, so you're just using me for my investigative skills, huh?" Ella joked, hoping the light banter would ease her agitated nerves.

"No! Of course not. This is all about the companionship. And the affection. And having the woman I love by my side. Before you, I hadn't been in a serious relationship in years. This is a nice change of pace for me."

"Same here. Especially considering the men of my past…"

The pair stepped inside the winery's vast lobby. A large crowd had already gathered, moving from table to table while sipping reds and nibbling cheeses.

Ella inhaled the fragrant scent of grape varieties. The aroma reminded her of that first visit to the vineyard. She'd been impressed with its shiny walnut interior, elegant leather furnishings and abstract oil paintings. Events were usually filled with overdressed women, and tonight was no exception. Ella had opted for a low-key look—a navy sheath dress, minimal makeup and a low bun. The last thing she wanted was to draw attention to herself. But after eyeing the majority of the attendees, who were decked out in showy designer gear, Ella realized she may stick out for appearing so plain.

"Welcome to Vincent Vineyard," a model-thin hostess said, handing them a glossy menu. "Here is a list of the wines that are being served tonight. Be sure to enter the raffle for a chance to win a bottle of our newest Cabernet Sauvignon."

Jake grabbed both menus and led Ella toward a discreet corner before pulling out his phone. "I'm gonna text Miles. See what time he and Charlotte are planning on getting here."

With her eyes glued to the pristine hardwood floor, Ella was careful not to make eye contact with anyone. She wondered whether any of the

Vincents had seen her yet. A quick scan of the room didn't reveal any familiar faces.

"Did Miles respond yet?" she asked, leaning into a high-top table while turning away from the crowd.

"Not yet. But the text just went through a second ago."

No sooner than Jake responded, Miles and Charlotte came strolling through the lobby. Charlotte was decked out in a fitted red tank dress and matching stilettos, while Miles and Jake appeared to have coordinated in advance as they were both wearing pale blue button-down shirts and European cut navy slacks.

Ella raised her hand in the air, waving frantically as relief set in. Charlotte blew her a kiss, then led Miles in their direction.

"Hey!" Ella said, throwing her arms around her sister. "I am so glad that you're here."

"Hi. Umm, didn't I just see you earlier today?"

Charlotte had no clue why being there for moral support meant so much to Ella. For the time being, she planned on keeping it that way.

"It's just nice having you here. That's all."

A server approached carrying a tray filled with wine flights and a charcuterie board. "Good evening, everyone. Would you like to try our collection of reds?"

"Absolutely," Jake told him. "What do we have here?"

"We've got our newest Cabernet Sauvignon, which is a wonderful blend of cherry and spices. If you enjoy rich, fruity flavors, then you'll love the Merlot. Our Zinfandel is a delicious blend of zesty, succulent strawberries. The Pinot Noir is one of my favorites thanks to its light, delicate blend of berries. And lastly, we've got our Malbec. People love the smoky plumlike flavor. All of the grape varieties used to produce these wines were grown right here at Vincent Vineyard. If you taste something you love, which I'm certain you will, please be sure to purchase a bottle before the end of the evening. Enjoy."

The moment the server was out of earshot, Jake turned to the group. "Now that's what I like to call a hard sell."

"Or maybe the man is just passionate about his wines," Miles said, picking up a glass of Zinfandel and taking a sip.

Charlotte gave him a side-eye. "Of course you'd start out with the strongest one."

"And you know it."

"Okay, now," Jake interjected. "Let's not lose sight of why we're here. Miles, have you spotted any of our unofficial persons of interest yet?"

"I have." He nodded at Charlotte, then Ella. "All right, ladies. You've both scoured the Vincent family's social media accounts and know what they look like. But let us give you a quick refresher. There's a portrait of our murder victim, Don Vincent, hanging over the fireplace. His wife, Claire, is standing to the left of it."

Ella leaned into Jake. "The thin older woman with the chignon, dressed in the black-and-white tweed Chanel suit?" she asked, as if she didn't already know.

"Bingo," Jake replied. "The two men she's speaking to are her sons. The oldest, Tyler, is the tall muscular one wearing the bright Burberry suit. His brother, Greer, is standing behind him. He's the short stubby guy with his hands in his pockets, dressed in a white polo shirt and black slacks."

"Well the difference between those two is clear," Charlotte said. "And they're at odds with one another, right?"

"Right," Miles confirmed. "Which is interesting, considering they worked together as a team to go against their father when he was still alive."

Covering his head with his hand, Jake turned away from the crowd. "Uh-oh. It looks like people are starting to notice us." He took a sip of Cabernet Sauvignon and popped a slice of smoked Gouda inside his mouth. "Just be cool. Act like you're here for the wine and hors d'oeuvres."

Ella followed his wandering gaze. Her eyes landed on Claire, who was staring in their direction.

She gasped, spinning around while praying she hadn't been spotted.

"You're fine, hon," Jake said, caressing her shoulder reassuringly. "Just because Miles and I work in law enforcement doesn't mean we shouldn't be here. Relax. Have some wine."

He pulled a glass of Pinot Noir from the wooden flight and handed it to her. Slowly pivoting, Ella glanced over at the fireplace. Claire was no longer there.

"So, back to the Vincents," Jake continued. "When it came to Don's sons, there was one thing that he did give in to. Don allowed them to arrange those group tours I'd mentioned at dinner, and build a visitors' area where guests could unwind over food, drinks and live music. But that was a decision he quickly grew to regret."

"Why is that?" Charlotte asked.

"Wait," Ella interjected. "I think I saw the answer to that question in one of the case files. Shortly before his death, didn't Don allow a bus full of visitors to come to the vineyard, and they ended up getting into a huge fight?"

"That's exactly right," Miles confirmed. "Not

only that, but Don got into a heated confrontation with a few of the guys who'd gotten drunk
and wandered off into the business offices. Of
course he thought they were looking to steal
trade secrets or something."

"Oh, wow," Charlotte uttered. "Whatever
came of the situation?"

"Not much," Jake told her. "Don reported the
incident to police. A couple of officers showed
up to the scene and investigated the situation.
But no one involved in the fight was talking,
and the guys who'd wandered into the office
area claimed they had gotten lost while searching for the men's room. No arrests were made."

Ella drained her glass, resisting the urge to
grab another. "Considering Don was killed
shortly after that incident, I think those visitors
need to be looked at again."

Nodding in agreement, Jake declared, "Trust
me, they are definitely on the list of folks who
will be questioned."

A sudden hush fell over the room. All eyes
turned toward the mosaic-tile floating staircase.
Two women stood at the top of the landing, but
only one stood out.

Jada Vincent.

Ella's entire body stiffened at the sight of her.
Tyler's stunning wife, whose sense of style was
just as flamboyant as his, glided down the stairs

in a pair of strappy six-inch heels. Her bone straight extensions appeared longer than the monogrammed Gucci dress clinging to her size-zero frame. Her fingers, which were adorned with a variety of blinding diamond rings, were tipped off with a set of pointy black acrylic nails.

Greer's wife, Faith, skulked closely behind her. She was at least a foot shorter and appeared much wider than her sister-in-law thanks to her run-over ballet flats and oversized gray shift dress.

"Okay, so…" Charlotte whispered in Ella's ear. "These two look familiar. Remind me who they are again?"

"Did you even *glance* at the case files and social media accounts Jake gave us to review?"

"Hey, talk to me after you become a new mother of a demanding mini diva who insists on constant cuddles and feedings and changing and—"

"All right, all right," Ella interrupted, just noticing the dark circles underneath Charlotte's eyes. "I get it." She discreetly pointed toward the staircase. "The woman in the Gucci dress is Jada Vincent, Tyler's wife. She's the sales director of Vincent Vineyard. The other woman is Faith Vincent, Greer's wife. She works as a sales and marketing rep."

"Geez. Talk about keeping it in the family. I

see they're both coupled up with the right brothers. Jada's flashy swag matches Tyler's to a T, and Faith's understated look goes right along with Greer's."

After polishing off a few slices of prosciutto, Jake wiped his mouth and grabbed his cell. "Listen, now that the wives have made their grand entrance, I think we should split up and gather some new intel. Let's go socialize. See what the crowd is buzzing about."

"And by crowd," Miles said to Ella and Charlotte, "Jake primarily means the members of the Vincent family."

"Exactly. Miles, Charlotte, why don't you two take the left side of the room while Ella and I take the right? We'll reconvene somewhere in the middle, let's say, in about thirty minutes?"

"Sounds like a plan, Chief." Miles took Charlotte's hand in his. "Happy mingling!"

The pangs of anxiety that had plagued Ella's stomach upon their arrival came back with a vengeance.

"Shall we?" Jake asked, offering her his arm.

She held onto him tighter than necessary, forcing her laden feet to follow him over to the jazz quartet playing near the back of the lobby.

"See the guy who Claire is talking to?" he asked, gesturing toward the terrace.

"I do. Doesn't he work for the vineyard?"

"He does. His name is Manuel Ruiz, and he manages this place. Word is Claire's been dumping all of her responsibilities off on him. So he knows the inner workings of the vineyard better than anyone. When we brought him in for questioning after Don's murder, he was extremely tight-lipped."

"Do you consider him a suspect?"

"Not at all. But I do think Manuel knows way more than what he's told us. Once I start bringing people in for questioning, he'll be one of the first."

Ella's heartbeat stuttered when Claire looked in their direction, then came sauntering over.

Please don't say anything...

"Chief Love," she said. "How nice to see you here. Last time we spoke, you were still working as a detective. Congratulations on your promotion to chief of police."

"Thank you, Mrs. Vincent. It's nice to see you as well. How have you been?"

Her eyelids, which were heavily embellished with thick false lashes, fluttered toward the floor. "I've been…okay, I guess. Some days are better than others. Knowing Don's killer is still out there makes me feel extremely uneasy—"

Claire paused, her voice cracking underneath the weight of her words. Manuel swooped in and wrapped his arm around her. "It's okay,

Mrs. Vincent. Now that Clemmington's got a new chief in place, let's hope we'll get some answers."

Manuel's bushy eyebrows shot up, accentuating the lines running across his leathery sunburned forehead. His chubby jowls trembled with emotion. Ella's chest tightened at the sight. For a brief second, she forgot about her own concerns. But when Claire's attention turned to her, they came rushing back.

"Oh!" Jake uttered, placing a hand on the small of Ella's back. "My apologies. I'm being rude. Mrs. Vincent, Mr. Ruiz, this is my girlfriend, Ella Bowman."

Shards of jagged nerves crawled from the soles of Ella's feet to the top of her spine. She extended her jittery hand, hoping Claire wouldn't remember her.

"It's nice to meet you, Mrs. Vincent."

"Pleasure to meet you as well, dear."

Claire's handshake was weak. Ella clenched her jaw, bracing herself for what was sure to come next. What would Jake say when he found out they'd met before? Under inappropriate circumstances, no less?

But instead of calling her out, Claire's dainty hand slipped from her grip. The faraway look in Claire's pale gray eyes told her everything she needed to know. Claire had no idea who she was.

The weight of relief almost knocked Ella to the ground. She'd gone unrecognized. At least for the time being...

"Testing, testing, one, two. Testing, one, two."

The crowd's attention shifted to Tyler, who was standing near the fireplace with a microphone in hand. The jazz quartet quieted their rendition of Frank Sinatra's "The Way You Look Tonight" before stopping completely.

"Jada, my love, could you please join me?" Tyler crooned.

His wife sashayed across the room, flinging her hair over her shoulder while giggling like a schoolgirl. Greer, who's fallen expression was riddled with annoyance, hovered in a corner while whispering in Faith's ear.

Sidling up to Claire, Manuel muttered, "Looks like somebody's upset that he's not included in the big speech."

"Well, the boys are just going to have to work things out among themselves."

"I'm sorry, Mrs. Vincent, but I disagree. Respectfully, of course. *You're* the one who's gonna have to work things out and make a decision. You know, choose which of your sons will take over as president of the vineyard."

Jake nudged Ella's arm and pointed toward his ear The pair moved in closer, listening in as Claire emitted a low moan.

"*Yes*," she drawled, crossing her arms over her frail chest. "I do plan on making a decision before one of them strangles the other to death and forces his way into the position."

"Ladies and gentlemen!" Tyler boomed. "Thank you so much for being here this evening. Tonight means the world to my family and I, and we're honored that you've chosen to join us. Since the death of my father, running Vincent Vineyard has been challenging to say the least. But my love of this business, along with the support of the Clemmington community, has helped keep me going."

Manuel rolled his eyes. "Why is this man speaking as if he's operating the vineyard on his own? Or at all for that matter?"

"*Please*," Claire hissed, swatting his shoulder. "Now is not the time. Any issues you have should be tabled for now and addressed at our Monday meeting."

"You let that oldest son of yours get away with murder, Mrs. Vincent. No pun intended. He's getting more and more out of control. You have got to do something about his behavior before he—"

"That's enough!" Claire spat so loudly that several guests turned and stared. She raised her hand, silently apologizing, then leaned toward

Manuel. "We will continue this conversation later, privately, inside my office."

"Yes, ma'am."

"Over time," Tyler continued, "I was able to convince my father to open his mind, which in turned helped to expand the Vincent Vineyard brand. He'd even agreed to allow visitor tours and build an outdoor deck shortly before his passing."

"*Passing*?" Manuel whisper-screamed. "The man was murdered!"

The steely look Claire shot at him immediately shut Manuel up.

Tyler strolled to the center of the room while wiping away invisible tears. "Speaking of Don's passing, I am proud to say that I have not allowed this tragedy to stop me from carrying on my father's legacy. The cloud surrounding his death illuminates with a silver lining. We have gathered here tonight to celebrate Vincent Vineyard's newest Cabernet Sauvignon. It was made from one of our more recent grape varieties, one which—which, uh…"

He hesitated, turning to his wife. "Jada, would you like to explain to our guests the details of this mouthwatering new offering?"

Her pointy heels screeched along the floor as she scrambled toward the mic. "Well, umm…this wine is delicious, guys! And it's extremely special to all of us because of—because of the, uh…"

A wave of murmurs rippled through the crowd. Guests peered at one another, their eyes wide and shoulders hunching in confusion.

"What an embarrassment!" Ella whispered to Jake.

The murmurs quieted as Greer trudged across the lobby, only to pick up again when Tyler snatched the mic from Jada.

"I guess it wouldn't be right for me to bask in *all* the celebratory glory," he quipped, a slight scowl peeking through his overly Botoxed face. "My brother, Greer, did play a part in producing this spectacular new wine. I'll let him take a few moments to tell you more about it."

Sweat poured from Greer's temples. He stood next to his brother, shuffling his feet from side to side while staring down at the floor. Without glancing in Tyler's direction, he grabbed the mic and stammered, "He—hello everyone."

"Oh, *Lord*," Claire snipped. "Please don't let my child stand up there and embarrass me."

"Just give him a minute," Manuel assured her. "You know your son. He usually needs time to gather himself."

After finally looking up at the crowd, Greer cleared his throat. "As my brother mentioned, it is an honor to be here celebrating with you. I am so pleased at how we've managed to keep my father's spirit alive through this amazing new Cabernet Sauvignon. It is a full-bodied, deliciously tart wine made from a hybrid grape, formed by the merging of Cabernet Franc and Sauvignon Blanc."

A soft smile spread across Claire's face. She held her hand to her mouth, whispering to Manuel, "Gold star for Greer!"

"See, I told you. The man is good. Good enough to be the president of Vincent Vineyard if you ask me. And before you even say it, I know. You don't want to make a decision just yet. But what it really boils down to is that Tyler's your favorite. However, you're not ready for that discussion. So I'll leave well enough alone."

Ella's eyes widened at Manuel's boldness. She held her breath, waiting for Claire's response. But the Vincent family matriarch remained silent, turning her attention back to Greer.

"Our wonderful servers will be passing around glasses of this savory full-bodied red. We hope you enjoy the powerful presence of chocolate, pepper, berries and oak. Please leave your feedback on the scorecards, and if you're inclined to take a bottle—"

"Or a case!" Tyler yelled out.

"...of wine home with you," Greer continued, ignoring his brother, "please do so. Thank you again for coming, and my family and I will be walking around to answer any questions you may have. Enjoy the rest of the evening."

He lowered his head humbly as the crowd broke into applause. Tyler pushed his way in front of Greer, as if the praise were for him.

"What a shame," Ella muttered. She eyed the exit, wondering if she'd be lucky enough to leave the tasting without running into the other family members.

As soon as the thought crossed her mind, Tyler and Jada came rushing over.

No, no, no!

They stopped in their tracks when Manuel began clapping loudly.

"Bravo, Greer! Wonderful speech! Simply *marvelous*!"

The crowd followed suit, their cheers growing louder. Tyler grabbed Jada's hand and dragged her back to the middle of the floor. He took a full bow, then raised his arm in the air as if he'd just won an Olympic gold medal. Jada appeared to understand the applause wasn't for her as she slowly backed away, sheepishly joining Greer's wife in the corner.

Claire nudged Manuel's arm. "See, now you're being an instigator."

"Not at all, Mrs. Vincent. I'm just giving props to the man who deserves them. But seriously?

You have got to make a decision and name one of your sons president. Who's it gonna be? *Tyler*," Manuel grumbled, his eyes rolling into the back of his head, "or my main man, Greer?"

Claire ignored him, lifting two glasses of wine off a passing server's tray.

"Thank you," Manuel said to her while reaching for a glass.

"Aht aht. These are both for me," she retorted before rushing off into the crowd.

"I'd better take advantage of this moment," Jake whispered to Ella just as Miles and Charlotte walked up.

"Mr. Ruiz," Jake said, "could I please talk to you for a minute?"

"Sure, Chief. I need to check on our VIP guests in the tasting room, but I've got a few minutes. What can I do for you?"

"I've been reviewing the case files from Don Vincent's murder investigation. My father insisted on conducting the majority of the interviews since he'd taken Mr. Vincent's death so personally."

Manuel's head dropped. He blinked rapidly, pressing his fingertips against his eyes.

"Are you all right, Mr. Ruiz?"

"Yep." He sniffled, scanning the room as if to see whether anyone was watching. "You being here just…just takes me back to the moment when Mr. Vincent was found stabbed to death and the fallout afterward. Accusations were being thrown around, business took a huge hit and the entire Vincent family has been at odds ever since. And who's in the middle of it all, fighting to hold everything together? *Me*."

"I understand that. And I'm sorry to hear it. I'm actually in the process of reopening Mr. Vincent's case. The family deserves answers, as do you and the rest of the Clemmington community."

"*The family*," Manuel snorted, grabbing a glass of wine off the nearest tray and downing it in a few gulps. "Good luck with that."

A commotion broke out on the other side of the room. As a crowd gathered, security stepped in attempting to break it up.

"Let's go," Jake said to Miles, setting off toward the brawl.

"No!" Manuel yelled, grabbing both officers and pulling them back. "Please, I respectfully ask that you stand down and let security handle it. I don't want our guests to see law enforcement confronting the brothers."

"The brothers?" Miles asked.

When the crowd broke, Jake realized it was Tyler and Greer who'd gotten into an altercation.

"Chief Love," Manuel said, "I'll take it from here. But I definitely want to speak with you about Mr. Vincent's murder. There are some things I didn't share after his death that I'm ready to reveal now. I'm tired of covering for people who should probably be behind bars."

Jake reached inside his pocket and pulled out a business card. "Call me. As soon as possible."

"You two need to cool off!" Claire yelled at her sons. "In my office. Now!"

Manuel shook Jake's hand, then slowly backed away. "I need to go and help diffuse this situation. I'll call you soon, Chief."

After he rushed off, Jake rejoined his group. "I think our work here is done. Why don't we head back to my place, exchange notes and discuss our next move?"

The words were barely out of his mouth before Ella linked arms with him and made a beeline for the exit. "Sounds like a plan."

"Charlotte and I got a lot of intel while eavesdropping on Jada and Faith," Miles affirmed.

"Same here," Ella said over her shoulder. "Except ours came from Claire and Manuel."

"Who knew this case would start taking shape at a wine tasting event of all places," Jake quipped.

Who knew I'd escape the event unscathed, Ella thought, ducking her head while rushing out the door.

Chapter Four

"How long have we been out here?" Charlotte panted.

"It hasn't even been twenty minutes, sis."

Ella rounded the corner of Clemmington High School's six-lane track, jogging at a slower pace than normal. Since having the baby, Charlotte had declared it her mission to shed the excess weight. She'd tapped Ella as her personal trainer. But getting Charlotte up and out of the house had proven to be challenging. Ella realized she had to come up with rewards in order to make it happen. That morning, she'd incentivized her sister with a banana smoothie and skinny latte before the day's workout.

"I shouldn't have drank all that coffee," Charlotte huffed. "I think I have to go to the restroom."

"*Again?* You just went five minutes ago!"

Charlotte shrugged, dipping off toward the

locker room. Ella grabbed her arm and dragged her back onto the track.

"Oh, no you don't. You are not slick. You're just trying to take another break. Once we hit the two and a half miles mark, you can slow down to a nicely paced walk. But until then, we have to keep moving."

"Ew, you are so annoying."

"Look, I'm just doing what you asked—trying to help get you back in shape in the event you decide to go back into law enforcement."

"If this is what it's gonna take, I'll opt to remain a stay-at-home mom."

"Yeah, right," Ella muttered. "I'll believe that when I see it. Once you feel comfortable leaving Ari with a nanny, you will be itching to get back on the force. Speaking of which, how would that work with you being a sergeant in River Valley and Miles being a detective here in Clemmington?"

"You know, I haven't even thought that far ahead. For now, I'm just focusing on enjoying motherhood and my engagement. I'll start thinking of wedding ideas once the time is right. But Miles and I have both been through so much. It's nice to concentrate on the good things in life without worry too much about the future. He's gonna be busy anyway now that he and Jake are reopening Don's cold case. But look, enough about me. How are things with you and Jake?"

The question curled Ella's lips into a blushing smile. "Good. *Really* good. I can honestly say that this is the best relationship I've ever been in. I'm talking no toxicity whatsoever. Being friends first really helped. We decided in the beginning to make communication a top priority since that's one of the things that our past relationships were lacking. So, we try our best to be open with one another, and honest…"

Ella's voice trailed off. A whirlwind of thoughts crashed her mind. The statement she'd just made was no longer true. Because she'd been far from honest with Jake as of late. Or anyone else for that matter, considering she had yet to reveal her connection to the Vincent family.

"Hey," Charlotte said, slowing down and nudging her arm. "What's wrong? Where did your mind go just now?"

Ella pulled away, unable to look Charlotte in the eye. She picked the pace back up and clapped her hands. "Come on, let's go! Don't try and distract me from the mission at hand. Keep it moving while we talk."

A loud grunt was all Ella heard behind her as Charlotte jogged to catch up.

"Is there something you're not telling me?"

Charlotte asked. "Because you've been acting a bit strange lately. Like something's bothering you, but you're holding it in."

"Nope," Ella lied, the reply shooting out of her mouth so fast that she was certain it sounded disingenuous. "There's nothing going on. My mind does tend to drift toward thoughts of Noel being the Numeric Serial Killer from time to time, and how you and I both almost lost our lives. But, I'm trying to work through all that."

"I still think it would do you some good to go to therapy. Talking with someone could really help. You might—"

"For the thousandth time," Ella interrupted, "I do not need therapy!"

"Okay!"

Ella spun around, not realizing she'd gained enough speed to leave her sister behind.

"I need a break, dammit," Charlotte continued, stumbling toward a nearby water fountain and taking a long drink. "Let's hit the bleachers and talk."

Here we go...

Ella took her time walking off the track. The soles of her black running shoes dragged across the rust-colored rubberized surface. Each freshly painted white line separating the lanes blurred as she thought of all the questions Charlotte may spring on her.

"Have a seat," Charlotte said, plopping down on a steel bench and banging her palm against the spot next to her.

The muscles in Ella's thighs tightened as she sat down. She stared straight ahead at the Go Clemmington Coyotes! sign planted across the track, already dreading the conversation before it had even begun.

"Hey," Charlotte began, "whatever came of the eyewitnesses and surveillance footage from that incident at the fall festival? Was Jake able to uncover anything that would help catch your attacker?"

"No, unfortunately. Jake did photo lineups for the eyewitnesses who claimed to have seen the suspect running through the corn maze. But none of them could make a definitive choice. As for the surveillance footage that security was supposed to turn over, they sent videos from the wrong day. By the time they tried to retrieve the footage from the night I was there, it had already been recorded over."

"Ugh, are you serious?"

"Yep."

"Well, don't lose hope, El. You know Jake is working hard on the case. Both yours and Don's. By the way, I love that he's including you in the investigation."

"I do too. It's sweet that he's so determined to keep me occupied while I'm on a work hiatus."

Charlotte slid toward the edge of the bleacher, stretching her calves against the row below her. "What do you think is really going on between those Vincent brothers? They have such a strange dynamic."

"They really do. And not only is it strange, but it's destructive. We know why though. They're both vying for that position of president and seem willing to do whatever it takes to get it."

"Even if it means killing for the position?" Charlotte asked.

"I believe so. Especially considering how they—"

You're talking too much!

"And their *wives*," Ella continued, quickly shifting gears. "That Jada seems just as bad a Tyler."

"Oh, for sure. Miles and I overheard her talking to some of the guests at the wine tasting. She is so superficial. All she did was brag about the new red convertible Maserati Tyler just bought her, their lake house in Tahoe and the private jet they're looking to purchase. Throughout the conversation, she kept waving her left hand in the air, flashing that obnoxious wedding ring set. In total, it looked to be about twenty carats!"

"What about Greer's wife, Faith? She seems pretty quiet. But pleasant."

Charlotte nodded in agreement. "She is, from what I could tell. One thing about her though. When it comes to Vincent Vineyard? The woman knows her stuff. I heard her speaking to some guests, and unlike Jada, Faith's conversation was all about the business. She rattled off so many facts about the grape varieties they grow, the distillery's new stainless steel fermentation vessel that doesn't add tannins to the wine, how the shape of a wine glass can affect the flavor. By the time we left the event, I felt like a sommelier!"

"Hmm, interesting. And how about Tyler's big speech? He had all the confidence in the world while addressing the crowd, but nothing prolific to share. Greer had to step in and save him from complete embarrassment."

"Then Tyler repaid him by starting a fight. It's terrible how Tyler seems to be the brother who's always in the forefront, when it should obviously be Greer. Same thing with Jada. She's the sales director, while Faith is a lower ranking sales rep. It should be the other way around."

Ella stood and propped her foot against the bench, stretching her hamstrings. "You know what they say. The squeaky wheel gets the oil. Greer and Faith need to step it up and be more vocal. He's clearly the better man for the job of president. But when Jake and I overheard their mother speaking with Manuel, it sounded as if she didn't want to play favorites by picking one son over the other. Manuel was trying to be the voice of reason and convince her that Greer is the best choice. But she was trying not to hear it."

"*Well*," Charlotte moaned as she dragged herself off the bleacher. "Lucky for us, we don't have to worry about helping Claire figure out better ways to run her business. We're just here to assist our men in finding her husband's killer. My money is on Tyler. He seems like the ruthless type who'd do anything to get ahead, whether he deserves the top spot or not."

"And that wife of his seems like she'd support him in any way she could if it meant beefing up their bank account." Ella broke into a slow jog. "Come on, let's get back to it. Two more laps around the track."

"Grr," Charlotte groaned, her sneakers scuffling against the asphalt. "And what are you gonna treat me to in return for these last laps?"

"How does a Chinese chicken salad from The Dearborn Grill sound?"

"Like something worth running for!" Charlotte picked up the pace, jogging alongside Ella to the rhythm of her steps. "So if you had to take a guess, who do you think is behind Don's murder?"

"Claire," Ella responded without hesitation.

"Really? Why is that?"

"Because technically, she had the most to gain. The vineyard is all hers now. Regardless of who takes over as president, Claire still holds the power. Not to mention if she was in fact having an affair, Don's death would mean she could continue doing so in peace—without worrying about getting busted or threats of a divorce. Plus, I don't know. There was something sketchy about her when she was talking to Manuel at the wine tasting. I just can't put my finger on it."

The urge to share her secret about the Vincents nipped at the back of Ella's throat. She swallowed it down, not ready to deal with the questioning. Or the judgment.

"THANKS AGAIN FOR LUNCH, SIS," Charlotte said as she and Ella exited The Dearborn Grill. "Next time, I'll treat."

"I'd love it if we could just get your workouts in without the promise of a reward. Especially when that reward is tied to food—"

A pinging cell phone stopped Ella mid-sentence.

"Oh, *sorry*!" Charlotte quipped, throwing her

hand in the air. "I can't hear you over all the loud beeping."

"Yeah, sure you can't."

While Charlotte checked her phone, Ella glanced down the block, contemplating whether she should walk back to Jake's place or go home with Charlotte and wait for him to pick her up after work.

As autumn settled upon Clemmington, the cozy vibe of the enchanting streets appeared more charming than usual. Leaves on the maidenhair and sweet gum trees had already transformed into eye-popping shades of gold, purple and red. Front porches were decorated with everything from pumpkins and gourds to orange mums and mini haystacks. Residents had switched out their tank tops and tees for oversized cable-knit sweaters. The fall season was in full swing, and Ella was looking forward to soaking up every bit of it—especially with Jake.

"Did you hear me?" Charlotte asked.

Ella spun around, realizing she hadn't heard a word her sister said.

"No, sorry. What'd you say?"

Charlotte propped her hand onto her hip. "Ma'am, what is it with you and all this drifting off into space? Are you sure you're okay?"

"Yes. I'm fine. I'm great, actually. I was just thinking about how happy I am being here in

Clemmington. Enjoying my favorite time of the year, being with the man I love…"

"And being here with your sister and niece too, right?"

"Of course! Now, what were you saying?"

"I was asking if you wanna come home with me and wait for Jake to pick you up. I can make us some hot chocolate and light the outdoor firepit, you can visit with Ari and shower her with kisses."

"Ooh, that sounds very tempting. But can I take a raincheck? I'd love to walk home and enjoy the sunset."

"*Walk?* But Jake's place is almost two miles away. I'm less than two minutes away. Wouldn't it make more sense for you to just wait for a ride home? Or I can drive you now if you need to get back sooner."

Ella reached out and embraced Charlotte tightly. "Thanks, sis. But no, I'm good. I'll call you when I get home."

"I've somehow found a way to take offense to this. I think what you're really trying to say is that you need to burn more calories because I slowed you down out there on the track this morning."

"Ha! That isn't even close to what I'm saying. But wait, now that you mention it…"

When Ella pulled away, she noticed a scowl on her sister's face.

"You do know that I was just joking, right?"

"Yeah, I know. I was just thinking about you walking home alone. Are you sure you'll be okay?"

Flashbacks of the attack inside the corn maze raced through Ella's mind.

Stop it. That was just a prank. Don't do that to yourself.

"Of course, Sergeant Bowman. I'll be fine."

"All right." Charlotte threw her a slight wave goodbye but didn't budge from the spot where she was standing.

Slowly backing away, Ella blew her a kiss. "I promise to call as soon as I get to Jake's. Now, don't worry about me. Go on home. I'm sure Ari misses you."

"Call me *as soon as* you get home!" Charlotte insisted before finally turning around and walking off.

Ella pulled out her wireless headphones and connected them to her phone. She tapped her "Autumn on the West Coast" playlist and strolled down the street to the rhythm of "September" by Earth, Wind and Fire.

A sweet vanilla-like scent filled the air. It sparked thoughts of Christmas. Ella took a look around, realizing it was coming from the balsam fir evergreens lining the businesses' doorways.

Before reaching the end of the block, she thought about stopping by the grocery store to pick up something for dinner. She and Jake had been ordering out constantly. Now that he'd officially reopened Don's cold case, Ella figured a home-cooked meal would do him some good.

She forged ahead, putting a little pep in her step as she hit the corner. Ella had stood at the intersection a couple of times before. Instinct told her to make a left and head down Hollow Lane. She peered into the distance, hoping she was going in the right direction.

Or you could just use Google Maps, Ella reminded herself. She opened the app and entered Fox & Sons Gourmet Market. Walking directions popped up. The store was twenty minutes away on foot.

Ugh...

Ella toyed with the idea of heading home and making do with whatever was in the refrigerator. But as far as she could remember, that consisted of a few eggs, a can of tuna, wilted arugula and a box of baking soda.

She envisioned surprising Jake with grilled lamb chops, scalloped potatoes, glazed carrots, strawberry cheesecake and a nice bottle of Bordeaux.

"Yep. Off to the store I go."

Continuing her trek down Hollow Lane, the street appeared fairly desolate—a far cry from busy Yellow Bell Avenue where the restaurant was located. Streetlights were few and far between, darkening the road as the sun quickly set. Front yards were empty as schoolchildren had already been ushered inside. Porch lights on the bungalow houses had yet to be turned on and only small bits of light crept through the looming tree branches.

The eerie scene sent Ella scurrying toward the end of the block. A barricade stood at the corner. Detour signs hung from each end with arrows pointing to the right. She checked Google Maps. The instructions told her to make a right turn. She tapped the screen and pulled up the detailed directions.

Construction up ahead. Reroute through Gateway Park.

Ella crept toward the park's iron gate. A narrow pathway surrounded by unkempt grass appeared. She pushed past the low hanging branches, marching along the trail while hoping that a snake wouldn't slither through the brush and attack.

The path led to a wide open field. Goalposts stood at either end, but there were no soccer players in sight. The park appeared empty. Ella hit the audio tab in Google Maps.

"Keep straight," the voice instructed. "In a half mile, turn right."

"A half mile!" Ella blurted out, her voice traveling through the wind up toward the darkening sky.

Okay, either you're in or you're out. Don't just stand here. Make a decision and go!

Without giving it another thought, Ella took off running. She breathed in through her nose and out through her mouth, laser focused on the other end of the park. If someone was going to come after her, they'd have to be one heck of a runner.

She stumbled, her ankle twisting on the uneven gray asphalt. But Ella took the hobble like a champ, straightening up and forging ahead without skipping a beat.

In two-three-four, out two-three-four, she internally chanted while inhaling and exhaling.

She removed her headphones and tossed them inside her pocket as strong winds threatened to snatch them up. Ella ignored the oddly shaped shadows bouncing off the path, appearing more like ghostly shadows than swaying tree limbs. The one thing she couldn't ignore, however, was the sound of footsteps thumping behind her.

Stinging pricks stabbed at her calves. A numbing fear threatened to send her tumbling to the ground.

"Do not turn around," she panted, struggling to pick up speed. But thoughts of being attacked again took hold of her muscles, subconsciously slowing her down.

The mix of chilled air and terror dampened Ella's eyes. Everything in front of her blurred. She blinked rapidly, a voice inside her head yelling, *No! Fight. Run faster!*

Ella managed to break through the angst weighing her down. She burst into a full sprint, wiping the tears from her eyes as three magic words appeared up ahead.

Gateway Park Exit.

"Yes!" she squealed. "Thank you!"

The footsteps that had been scuffling behind her grew distant. She pushed open the park's iron gate and ran out, then boldly turned around to see who'd been following her.

A man who looked to be at least eighty years old appeared in the near distance. He was hunched over, barely making his way along the path. He waved at Ella, then held his hands to his mouth.

"Nice sprint, young lady! I remember back when I was able to run like that. Nowadays I'm just glad my legs still work!"

"Thank you!" Ella whimpered with relief, giving him a thumbs-up before falling against a brick column.

You're good. Everything's fine. You've just gotta stop letting your imagination run wild.

"Keep straight," the voice directions in Google Maps instructed. "In thirty feet, your destination will be on the right."

Ella stretched her back, then headed toward the store, emitting an exhilarating whoop when Fox & Sons finally came into view. She sent Charlotte a text, letting her know she'd stopped by the grocery store and asking if she wouldn't mind picking her up and taking her home.

"Because there is no way in hell I'm walking back to Jake's from here."

Within seconds, her phone buzzed. Ella expected to see a response from her sister. But instead, an email popped up from anonymous@anonymous.com.

What in the world is this...

She swiped open the message.

You Are One Bold Bitch, the subject read.

The phone almost fell from Ella's hand. She squeezed her eyes shut, willing herself to read the message.

Come on. You can do this. You have to.

Her eyelids gradually lifted as she scanned the bold letters, typed in all caps.

FIRST YOU HAVE THE AUDACITY TO SHOW UP AT VINCENT VINEYARD, THEN YOU FIND THE NERVE TO STRUT THROUGH MY NEIGHBORHOOD, AND MY PARK? ALONE?? YOU'D BETTER BE GLAD THAT OLD MAN CAME OUTTA NOWHERE. HE SAVED YOUR LIFE. JUST LIKE THAT SECURITY GUARD DID INSIDE THE CORN MAZE. BUT TRUST ME. NEXT TIME, YOU WON'T BE SO LUCKY. ELLA BOWMAN, YOU ARE NOT IN NEVADA ANYMORE. HERE IN CLEMMINGTON, THE ODDS WILL NEVER BE IN YOUR FAVOR...

Chapter Five

Jake sped through Vincent Vineyard's parking lot and pulled into a space near the entrance.

"We're late," he said to Miles.

"Yeah, that's because we shouldn't be here. Tyler was supposed to meet us at the station for questioning. Not on his turf, where he'll be cool and calm in his own element."

"Not necessarily," Jake replied, leading the way toward the door. "Maybe he'll be nervous since we're at the scene where his father was murdered. If Tyler did have anything to do with Don's death, I expect him to be extremely uneasy once he finds out we're obtaining a search warrant."

"True. Either way, I just hope we get some answers."

The officers entered the winery. Tyler and Jada were standing in the middle of the lobby, dressed in matching monogrammed Louis Vuitton outfits.

"These two…" Miles muttered under his breath.

"Gentlemen!" Tyler boomed, approaching the men with open arms. "Welcome back to Vincent Vineyard. Can I get you two anything? A glass of Merlot? Pinot Noir? Our fabulous new Cabernet Sauvignon, perhaps?"

"Thank you, Mr. Vincent," Jake responded, "but Detective Love and I are on duty."

Waving him off, Tyler grunted, "Ahh, who cares about the rules? You're among friends. I won't tell if you won't. Right, hon?"

He pivoted on the heels of his shiny black snakeskin oxfords, stopping in front of Jada.

"That's right, babe," she gushed through a mouth full of stark white veneers. "So what's it gonna be, fellas? I'll bring out whatever you want."

"We're good, thanks," Miles reiterated sternly. "Mr. Vincent, is there somewhere we can talk? Privately?"

Tyler's arms fell by his side as his entire body deflated. "Yeah, we can meet in my office. Jada, could you please excuse us?"

"Of course. But before you all go…" She paused, reaching for Jake's chest. "Are you *sure* I can't get you two a glass of—"

"*Jada*!" Tyler snapped so loudly that she

almost jumped out of her shoes. "Excuse us. *Please*. I'll circle back with you later."

Her lower lip trembled as she stormed off, her stilettos screeching against the hardwood floors.

"You're leaving scratches!" Tyler yelled to her back. "Pick up your feet!" He balled his right hand inside the left and cracked his knuckles. "Gentlemen, follow me. I'll show you to my office."

Jake and Miles threw one another exasperated glances on the way there.

"So, Chief Love, you were pretty vague when we spoke on the phone about this meeting. What exactly is it you'd like to speak with me about?"

"We were hoping to discuss your father's murder, in detail. Since you're the one who found his body, we want you to walk us through exactly what happened."

"But I already told your father everything I knew back when he was investigating the case."

"We're well aware of that," Miles interjected. "But now that a year has passed and some of the shock has worn off, you may remember something that slipped your mind during the initial investigation."

Tyler stopped at the bottom of the staircase. "I can guarantee you that this situation is just as traumatizing now as it was back when it first occurred."

Miles peered at him, slowly nodding his head. "I understand."

"However, you may be right. I'm willing to talk about that day. At least what I can remember of it."

As Tyler headed up the stairs, Jake held Miles back.

"Mr. Vincent?" the chief said.

"Yes?"

"Instead of talking us through that day, would you be willing to walk us through it instead?"

"What do you mean?"

"Are you up for taking us out to the grape fields and retracing your steps, showing us exactly what happened when you found your father's body?"

An uncomfortable silence filled the lobby. Tyler's eyes darted from Jake and Miles to the front door, as if he were contemplating making a run for it.

"Look, if you think that would be too much for you to do—"

"Nope," Tyler interrupted, bouncing back down the stairs. "That's not it. I just—this won't be easy. I'm still suffering from PTSD over the whole ordeal." He squared his broad gym-honed shoulders and readjusted the lapel on his fitted blazer. "But I'm up for it. Let's do this."

Faux confidence burst from his feet as Tyler

led them onto the terrace. Jake stepped outside, inhaling the fragrant scent of grapevine flowers. Yellow beams of light streamed from the sky, fading in between layers of fog that had rolled in off the Pacific Ocean. The vast rows of grapes were barely visible underneath the haze.

"Wow, this is stunning," Miles said. "How large is the field?"

"Seventy-two acres," Tyler uttered, staring out at the gentle slopes. "Dad was so proud of what he'd built. From harvesting the grapes to bottling the wine, that man knew how to do it all. He could've run this place alone if he had to. For a short time, right after purchasing it, he actually did—"

When Tyler's voice wavered, Jake placed a hand on his shoulder. "I'm so sorry. Are you sure you're up for this? We can talk in your office if you think that would be easier."

"Nope. I'm up for this. Let's go."

The brothers followed him along the dirt paths tucked between wide rows of grapevines. Gusts of wind sent billows of dust swirling around Tyler's designer ostrich shoes. He didn't seem to care. He was the type who'd toss them in the garbage and order a new pair.

"I found my father's body up ahead," he mumbled, pointing toward an area filled with clusters of small tightly packed purple grapes. "In the middle of his beloved Pinot Noir vines. He was having so much trouble with that variety last year. They were beginning to rot, which, according to Greer, was due to the grapes' thin skin. I kept telling my dad to just let it go. We were losing a ton of money. Pinot Noir isn't even one of our bestsellers. But *no*. That man was determined to make it work. All because Alan Monroe's winery had produced a successful line of it."

Jake was tempted to ask why he was so concerned with the vineyard's profits rather than his father's death. But he refrained, making a mental note of it instead.

"What time did you arrive at the vineyard that day, Mr. Vincent?" the chief asked.

"Umm…at around 11:00 a.m."

"Is that what time you normally arrive?"

"Yes, for the most part. My father would usually get here at around 7:00 a.m. And Greer comes in soon after, at about 7:30 a.m. or so."

"I guess this is a question I could ask Greer when we speak to him," Miles said, "but is there any reason he didn't find your father's body first, since he was here hours before you'd arrived?"

"*Humph*," Jake huffed, scratching his head in feigned confusion. "Greer claimed he was in the distillery most of the morning, supervising the installation of the new wine press. Key word, *claimed*."

"Duly noted," Jake said, opening the Notes app on his cell phone and typing in his exact words. "And this area here is the precise location of where the body was found?"

Tyler's head fell. He closed his eyes, barely nodding while mouthing the word *yes*.

Despite having plenty of photos from the crime scene inside the case file, Jake used his phone to snap several more. "Can you tell me what condition your father was in when you saw him?"

"He, uh…he was lying on his side, with his back to me. I ran to him, thinking that he may have fallen out under the hot sun, or even had a heart attack. But when I turned him over, there was a pool of blood gathered beneath his body. His shirt was soaked, right in the chest area. When I saw that, I thought a coyote may have attacked him, or he'd fallen into one of the wooden posts. I just couldn't wrap my mind around the thought of my father being killed."

"So it never occurred to you that a knife could've done that damage? Or a bullet even?"

"No," Tyler deadpanned, his left eyelid twitching uncontrollably.

"What did you do after finding your father?"

"I yelled for help. I didn't have my cell phone

on me at the time. After a while, I realized no one could hear me all the way out here. I hated leaving my father alone. But I had to call 9-1-1. So, that's what I did. Went straight to my office and called the authorities."

Miles pulled a small notepad from his blazer pocket and flipped through several pages. "If I can recall correctly, when your wife was questioned, she stated that you went running to *her* office, saying you'd found your father's body. This occurred before 9-1-1 was called. Case notes also state that your wife was the one who actually made the 9-1-1 call."

Tyler pulled a monogrammed handkerchief from his pocket and dabbed it over his dampening face. "That could be the case. I'm not sure, Detective. It's been a long time since all that went down. I know you don't expect me to remember every single little detail."

"No," Jake replied. "We don't. But the problem is, that's not what we'd consider a little detail. Not being able to recall whether you were the one who dialed 9-1-1 is pretty significant—"

"Hold on," Tyler interrupted, backing away from the officers. "Did you all come out here to gain new insight? Or accuse me of murder? Because if it's the latter, I'm going to have to ask you to leave and not speak to me again until my attorney is present."

His defensiveness etched a bright red flag into Jake's brain.

Defuse the situation before he lawyers up...

"That's not the case at all, Mr. Vincent," Jake insisted. "Our only goal is to gather as much information as possible and bring justice to your family."

"Yeah, right," Tyler rebutted. "Need I remind you that it was Clemmington PD who dropped the ball on finding my father's killer. Not me. So please refrain from speaking to me in that accusatory tone, inside *my* place of business, and asking incriminating questions while my lawyer isn't here."

"Again, that was not my intention—"

"*Also,*" Tyler interrupted, "I do understand that you're the new chief of police. But don't let that go to your head. Trying too hard to score a touchdown could cause you to fumble the ball, *rookie.*"

Jake's entire body stiffened. His hands rolled into tight fists as the urge to square up left him shaking.

Raising his watch in the air, Tyler eyed the time. "Sorry to cut this conversation short, or should I say, interrogation?"

"No," Miles replied flatly. "You had it right the first time."

"Okay, well, sorry to cut this *conversation*

short, but according to my Hublot Unico, I've got a meeting to get to. A major wine distributor's coming in, and I can't be late. God forbid I allow Greer to handle it on his own. He'd bomb it before the presentation even got started. Yet another reason I should've been named president a long time ago…"

Before either of the brothers could respond, Tyler had already set off toward the main building.

"What an obnoxious piece of—"

Jake gripped Miles's shoulder, stopping him mid-sentence. "Keep your cool, man. Let's just continue to give this guy enough room to incriminate himself."

The brothers peered ahead, watching as Tyler climbed the marble stairs two at a time while typing away on his cell phone.

"What's the next order of business, Chief?" Miles asked.

"Next order of business? We need to talk to Greer."

Chapter Six

Ella carried one of Don Vincent's case files over to the dining room table, careful not to slip on the freshly waxed floors. She glanced at the clock. It was after 6:30 p.m. Jake would be home any minute.

She cracked open the oven door, checking on the Cornish hens. A whiff of the roasting meat drifted through the air, along with hints of the bell peppers, white mushrooms and sweet yellow onions. After lowering the temperature, she shut the door and sat down at the table, sipping a cup of herbal tea while taking a quick look around.

Jake lived in an industrial style two-bedroom loft located in a refurbished building once used to manufacture medical equipment. Large arched windows allowed in plenty of sunlight, while exposed brick, walnut flooring and timber support beams gave the place a sexy masculine feel. The gourmet kitchen and spa bathroom were a far cry from her modest one-bedroom apartment back home, making her feel as though she were living in the lap of luxury.

I could get used to this, Ella thought the moment she'd walked through the door.

Since reopening Don's cold case, Jake's loft had turned into a war room of sorts. Boxes, files, photos and reports were strewn everywhere. Ella had grown tired of the clutter and managed to gather it all inside the office, vowing to try to maintain some semblance of order as she assisted in the investigation.

But keeping his place intact had become the least of her concerns. After the scare at the park and subsequent email, Ella was struggling to figure out how to tell Jake what was going on. The longer she waited, the wearier she grew. Don's investigation was in full swing. Not only was the Vincent family aware of it, but so was the entire Clemmington community. The news made the front page of *The Daily Herald* earlier that week, the headline reading, *New Police Chief Reopens the Case His Father Couldn't Solve*.

The title was triggering for Kennedy, making him feel as though he'd failed the community despite putting in over thirty-five otherwise successful years on the force. As for Jake, the pressure to solve the case went from zero to one hundred within a matter of days. Ella could already see the signs of stress. He hadn't been eating regularly, and sleep had become challenging since he couldn't turn off his brain at night. Pouring over the same case files time and time again in hopes of uncovering missed details wasn't helping matters.

If Ella told Jake the secret she'd been keeping, it would send him over the edge and probably end their relationship. The mere thought sent pangs of devastation crashing through her head.

Just keep it to yourself. At least for the time being...

In the midst of all the madness, Ella had managed to find one solid lead during her investigation. Buried within a stack of crime scene photos were notes taken the day a group of tourists fought at Vincent Vineyard, shortly before Don's death. Ella pulled the names of the men involved and did an online search. She discovered that one of them had a criminal history.

Ben Foray had been arrested in San Diego on charges of forgery, robbery and false imprisonment a few months prior to the brawl. The accuser, whose identity had been kept anonymous, opted not to press charges. Ben walked away a free man.

Five months after the vineyard incident, he was arrested again and charged with corporal injury to a spouse or intimate partner. The most recent news article reported that Ben was out on bail and awaiting trial. Ella thought it would be a good idea to give him another look.

The sound of Jake's keys jiggling outside the door sent a thrill through Ella that jolted her toward the door. She threw her arms around him the moment he walked inside, greeting him with a warm embrace and lingering kiss.

"Welcome home, babe," she murmured.

"Hey you," he said, chuckling in between kisses. "To what do I owe all this love and affection?"

"Just being the good man that you are. That's all."

Jake slid his hand in hers and glanced around the loft. "Wow. It looks great in here. What did you do, hire a cleaning service? And what is that delicious aroma coming from the kitchen?"

"First, no, I didn't hire a cleaning service. I straightened this place up all by myself after realizing I'd made a mess of it with all the boxes and case files. Second, I prepared a nice home-cooked meal for you since you've been working so hard. Seems as if you needed a little pick-me-up."

"That I did. And in turn, I think *you* deserve a special thank-you."

Ella's body grew warm as Jake ran his fingertips along the small of her back. She leaned into him, her lips tasting traces of cedar cologne lingering on his neck. He pulled her closer, kissing her deeper. As he slowly steered her toward the bedroom, Ella stopped, attempting to lead him in the opposite direction.

"Oh, no you don't," she said, laughing softly. "Didn't you get enough of that this morning?"

"Is that a real question?" Jake's gaze roamed her curvaceous figure, which was on full display in a fitted off-white romper. "Let me be clear about one thing. I can *never* get enough of that."

"You'd better cut it out," Ella warned playfully.

"All right, fine. If you're not gonna indulge me in the bedroom, the least you could do is feed me. What are we having?"

"Roasted Cornish hens, lemon herb quinoa and a shaved Parmesan arugula salad with homemade vinaigrette dressing."

"Mmm, sounds amazing." Jake followed Ella into the kitchen and washed up at the sink, then poured two glasses of wine. The articles she'd printed were still scattered across the table. He took a seat and thumbed through each of them. "What's all this?"

"That, my love, is what I'd like to call a hot new lead in the investigation."

"Ooh, really? Tell me more, Detective Bowman."

"While I was scanning the case files, I came across a stack of photos from the crime scene. Stuck in between them were notes that were taken after the fight incident at the vineyard. The articles you're holding are about one of the men who'd been involved. His name is Ben Foray. Does it ring a bell?"

Peering down at the man's photo, Jake shook his head. "No, it doesn't. But we questioned those guys so briefly. No one was hurt during the scuffle, and there wasn't any damage done to the vineyard. I do remember Don wanting to press charges, but Tyler and Greer convinced him not to do so. Especially Tyler. Neither he nor Greer wanted the negative attention. Claire ended up taking the side of her sons. So, despite his better judgment, Don decided to drop it."

"Well, what do you think? Judging by those charges Ben's been hit with in recent months, wouldn't it be worth bringing him back in for questioning?"

"Absolutely. Thank you. This was an awesome discovery. And it's so ironic…"

"What do you mean?"

"I put a call in to Manuel yesterday asking when we could talk. He said he'd come down to the station, because he didn't want to discuss the case at the vineyard. Problem is, he's busy as hell trying to help Greer keep the place up and running smoothly."

"No surprise there. Seems like Claire and

Tyler are too focused on their own agendas to get any work done."

"Exactly. So Manuel and I are in the process of getting a meeting on the calendar. In the meantime, I asked him to send me the surveillance footage from that day the fight broke out. He emailed it over yesterday. But I've been so busy that I haven't had a chance to look at it yet."

"Wait, you've already got the footage in your possession?"

"I do."

"That's great! Why don't we take a look at it over dinner?"

"Good idea," Jake said, pulling his laptop from his brown leather messenger bag.

Ella rushed to prepare their plates, barely sitting down before honing in on the computer screen. She held her breath as Jake pulled up his email. "I cannot believe I'm actually a part of this investigation. Well, *unofficially*, but still. Is it wrong for me to be this excited?"

"No, not at all. Do you know how exhilarating it is to solve a case? You're supposed to be excited. That's why being a member of law enforcement is so fulfilling." He turned the laptop in her direction and opened Manuel's message. "Okay, here we go."

Ella scanned the email. "All right, so Manuel has identified the men in the video by their hair and outfits. Ben Foray has a shoulder-length brown mullet and is wearing a dark green polo shirt, Mitch Wilkerson is in the white button-down and has a short blond crew cut and Dylan Lee is bald, dressed in a black T-shirt. Got it?"

"Got it."

There were two videos attached. Jake double-clicked on the first one. A new screen popped up. He pressed Play.

The upstairs area of the vineyard's main building appeared. Within seconds, three men could be seen creeping up the staircase. The first had long curly hair, the second had a blond crew cut and the third was bald.

"Okay, our culprits have been made their grand entrance," Jake said.

"And look at them, opening all the office doors, peeking inside. The audacity..."

The pair watched closely as the men approached a door at the end of the hallway, cracked it open then went inside.

"The police report stated that Don caught these guys in his office," Ella confirmed. "I'm wondering if that's it."

"If it is, then Don should be showing up any second now. Let's keep watching."

Two minutes passed before Don came into the frame. Manuel was by his side, along with a man wearing a black chauffeur hat and blazer.

"That's the tour bus driver walking with Don and Manuel," Jake said.

Ella leaned in closer, watching as Manuel threw open each door lining the hallway. When he reached the corner office, Don stormed inside. Manuel followed him while the driver stood in the doorway.

"Uh-oh," she said, her eyes widening. "I'm almost afraid to see what's about to happen next."

No sooner than the words were out of her mouth, the three visitors came charging out of the office. The driver tried to stop them, but they tore away from his reach and flew down the hallway. Right before Ben went out of frame, an envelope fell from his pocket. He quickly bent down and grabbed it, barely escaping the driver's grasp before jetting off. Then, the screen went blank.

"*Whoa*," Ella gasped. "Did you see what I just saw?"

"I sure did."

"I wonder what was inside of that envelope."

"Trust me, that'll be one of the first things I ask Ben when I question him."

Jake clicked on the second video. Another screen popped up. This time, the east side of the vineyard appeared, where the visitor area was located. A billowing tan awning hovered above a stone U-shaped bar. Cushioned cream stools and mahogany table sets lined the perimeter. Within seconds, a group of people emerged.

Ella swallowed a forkful of quinoa, then sipped her drink, watching as a few couples took seats at the bar. Larger groups sat at the tables while servers appeared carrying trays filled with wine glasses and charcuterie boards.

Soon after, Mitch and Dylan came into view, shuffling sheepishly toward the visitor area. Mitch's head hung low while Dylan's hands were stuffed inside his tapered chinos. When Ben resurfaced, his arms were waving wildly through the air as he gestured toward Don and Manuel, who reappeared moments later.

"That Ben is a problem, isn't he?" Ella asked.

"Problem might be an understatement. Judging by what I'm seeing here, on top of everything you shared regarding his criminal history, I need to bring him in for questioning ASAP. The police report from this incident didn't include all these details."

"Tyler and Greer probably downplayed everything since they didn't want to press charges. Whatever it takes to shine a positive light on the vineyard and keep profits rolling in, right?"

"Apparently so." Jake polished off the last of his Cornish hen and wiped his mouth. "On a side note, this meal is fantastic, babe."

"Thank you. I'm glad you're enjoying it. Wait,

look!" Ella pulled the computer closer as Ben pointed his finger in Don's face. "We've got action. Mayhem is about to ensue in five, four, three, two—"

Before she hit one, Don flung Ben's arm in the opposite direction. Ben lunged forward with his fists in the air. Manuel stepped in just in time, blocking a blow that almost connected with Don's jaw.

"Where in the hell are Tyler and Greer?" Jake asked right before both sons emerged. Tyler grabbed Ben, helping Manuel hold him off while Greer led his father back inside the main building. The bus driver kept Mitch and Dylan at bay as the rest of the guests looked on in horror.

Ella shook her head, stabbing at a piece of arugula. "Who would've thought that this type of chaos would take place at such a nice establishment?"

"Well, it's to be expected when you've got criminals and their cronies on your property. Maybe this is one of the reasons why Don didn't want the visitor area to be built in the first place."

Once the Vincent men and Ben were out of the frame, the video cut off.

"I guess I'll be adding a few more persons of interest to my list," Jake said, downing the last of his wine. "I can't thank you enough for finding those notes. And doing the research on Ben. *And* reviewing this surveillance footage with me. This has been a good night. One that I really needed."

"I think we both really needed it."

The smile on Jake's face faded. He stared off into the living room, his mind clearly roaming into heavier territory.

"And it's not over yet," Ella said, giving his hand an affectionate squeeze before clearing the dishes. "Wait until you see what's for dessert."

Jake pivoted, watching as she walked toward the sink. "I can already see what's for dessert. And I'm giving it five stars in advance."

"I'm saving *that* dessert for later. But in the meantime, how about you try some of this?"

"Mmm," he breathed at the sight of a pumpkin meringue pie. "How did you find out about my obsession with Rita's famous pumpkin pie?"

"Through Miles, of course. Lucky for you, Rita added her seasonal fall desserts to the menu earlier this week. I know you've been having a rough go of things since taking on Don's case. So, I wanted to do something special for you tonight."

"And that you did. Thank you."

Jake walked over and brought Ella close, caressing her neck with his lips.

"Mmm, that tickles," she moaned as the nuzzling turned into deep kisses.

He grabbed her by the waist and whispered,

"Let's save the pie for later. There's something tastier that I've gotta have. *Right* now."

"Lead the way," Ella said before following him to the bedroom.

When they reached the doorway, Jake paused. "Oh, by the way, you're gonna have to get yourself a nice cocktail dress. If you don't have one already."

"Oh, really? What's the occasion?"

"I received an invitation to a charity event being held by the Vincent family. And you're my plus-one."

"Wait. You…you received *what*?"

"An invitation to a fundraiser being thrown by the Vincents. It's in support of underprivileged students who don't have the funds to pay for college. I usually go every year. After the way things went down when Miles and I met with Tyler, I honestly didn't expect to be invited. But my guess is that Claire's in charge of the guest list."

Ella barely heard a word that Jake had spoken. She was too wrapped up in the thought of having to face the Vincent family yet again.

Chapter Seven

Ella checked her reflection in the full-length mirror hanging behind the bedroom door one last time. Her strapless velvet burgundy dress hugged every curve. She'd styled her hair into a low bun and molded her bangs into sleek body waves. Her makeup was simple—golden nudes with a deep matte red lipstick. But the highlight of the entire look was her red and black ombré-feathered mask, trimmed in sparkling black sequins.

When Jake first told her about the Vincents' charity event, he was so busy trying to get her inside the bedroom that he'd failed to mention the fundraiser's masquerade theme. It was the one saving grace that would help Ella blend into the crowd while observing the family.

"El!" Jake called out from the living room. "You ready, babe? We're gonna be late. I don't wanna miss the auction. I have got to put in my bid on those Lakers tickets and the players' meet and greet afterward."

"I'm coming!" Ella gave herself one last glance before grabbing her black satin clutch and heading out.

"*Phew phew,*" Jake whistled, embracing her the moment she stepped foot inside the living room. "Woman, don't make me skip out on this event altogether and take you right back into that bedroom. You look…*phenomenal*. I'm feeling a little subpar dressed in this plain ole black suit."

"Subpar? Please. You'll be the most handsome man there. However, if there *is* a way for you to mail in your donation so that we can skip the event, I'd be down with that."

Jake chuckled, not realizing Ella was dead serious.

"Not a chance," he told her. "If nothing else, I wanna show you off. Let the entire town of Clemmington see just how beautiful my lady is."

The response sparked a burning dread that simmered inside Ella's gut.

You've got your mask. You'll be fine, she told herself on the way out the door.

But there was one small factor Ella had forgotten. Everyone knew that she was dating Jake. When they saw him, they'd know it was her by his side—especially after he'd refused to wear a mask.

Just stay low-key and keep your head down...

Ella slid inside the car and immediately rolled down the window, hoping the cool night air would garner some relief. When Jake turned on a smooth jazz satellite station, she closed her eyes and swayed to the music.

Don't worry about tonight. All will be well.

A deep pothole jolted her eyes open. Ella stared out the window. Jake had just made a right turn down the wrong street. "Wait, where are we going? Isn't Vincent Vineyard in the opposite direction?"

"It is. But the charity event isn't being held there. It's at the Hidden Treasure Casino."

"Really? I don't remember you mentioning that."

Jake reached over and laced his fingers within hers. "Sorry. Must've slipped my mind. I've been so focused on Don's investigation that I'm having trouble remembering whether I'm coming or going."

Ella sank down into her seat, relaxing against the backrest. Relief set in at the thought of avoiding the vineyard. Guests at a casino would be spread all around the gaming floor, making it easier for her to blend in with the crowd.

Bright lights shone up ahead as they approached Hidden Treasure. Jake slowed down, eyeing the long valet line filled with luxury cars.

"I see the Vincents have brought out the who's who among Clemmington," Ella murmured, staring out at the throngs of elaborately dressed attendees crowding the entrance.

"As they do every year. That wait for the valet is probably gonna take forever. I'd better park in the garage. I'll drop you off in front first. Don't think I didn't notice how high those sexy heels are you're wearing. I don't want your feet to start hurting."

"That's sweet of you. But these shoes are pretty comfortable. Go on to the lot. I'll walk back with you."

"Are you sure?"

"I'm positive."

Jake proceeded to the garage, driving up the ramp until they reached the top floor. "It is a packed house tonight. But that's a good thing. The bigger the turnout, the bigger the endowment."

"Uh-huh," Ella muttered, barely listening as a bout of anxiety tightened her chest.

After pulling into a space and helping her out of the car, Jake took a step back, ogling Ella from head to toe. "Whew! Did I mention how beautiful you look tonight?"

"You did. And thank you again." She glanced down at his hand. It was wrapped in black satin. "What is that you're holding?"

Unwinding the unidentified object, he placed it over his face, secured it behind his head and turned to her.

"It's my swashbuckling mask."

"A *mask*? But I thought you weren't going to wear one."

"I wasn't. However, tonight is for a good cause. Since I'm the chief of police, I figured the least I could do is follow the event rules."

"Well, I'm glad you did. You look great." Ella looped her arm within his. "So great that you just might have to keep that on when we get home."

"Ooh, I think I like the sound of that…"

Ella slipped on her mask before they entered the elevator. When the doors opened onto level one, they squeezed their way out onto the crowded sidewalk and headed toward the casino.

"Wow, this place is nice," she said, staring up at the gold awning and rolling spotlights shining down on the bright red carpet. "Reminds me of Las Vegas."

The thought of her home state reminded Ella of the threatening message she'd received after leaving Gateway Park.

You are not in Nevada anymore. Here in Clemmington, the odds will never be in your favor…

She tightened her grip on Jake's arm. He

glided his hand over hers, their fingers instinctively intertwining. The warmth of his touch put her mind at ease, at least for the time being.

Photographers stood outside the casino's grand entryway, snapping candid pictures of guests as they strolled inside. Frank Sinatra's "Luck Be a Lady" blared from multiple speakers hanging from the revolving doorways.

The moment Ella and Jake hit the gaming floor, the music was drowned out by ringing slot machines and cheering gamblers. Crowds were gathered around blackjack, roulette and poker tables. The energy was electrifying as dealers shuffled cards, bartenders poured craft cocktails and servers passed around glasses of Vincent Vineyard wine.

"What are we drinking tonight?" Jake asked right before they were approached by a couple.

Ella stopped so abruptly that her heel snagged against the pale gold carpet. Had she not been holding onto Jake, she would've stumbled to the floor. She stared down at her feet, barely looking at the pair, whose faces were covered in crystal Venetian masks.

Panic set in. Was it Tyler and Jada? Or maybe Greer and Faith?

"My, oh, my," Ella heard Jake say. "You two really went all out, didn't you? If there's a prize for best masks, you'll definitely win first place."

"And if that prize consists of a case of wine," a familiar voice responded, "we'll take it!"

Someone nudged Ella's shoulder. "What is wrong with you? Why are you just standing there, hiding behind Jake without even saying hello? Could you be any more rude?"

Slowly raising her eyes, Ella grinned sheepishly after realizing it was Charlotte and Miles.

"Oh, sorry!" she squealed, embarrassment flaming her skin as she hugged her sister. "You look great. I'm loving your satin green dress. And those masks. Where'd you get them?"

"Miles and I scoured the internet for these. We found them at a little boutique in New Orleans that specializes in Mardi Gras costumes."

"Well, they look amazing." Ella quickly turned to Jake, feeling as though they were on full display at the casino entrance. "Should we go grab a drink? Then play some slots or a little blackjack?"

"All the above. Charlotte, Miles, would you two like to join us, or are you gonna hit the craps table first, which is all Miles has been talking about for days?"

"I'd love a drink," Charlotte said. "Miles has plenty of time to blow our money playing craps. Let's not encourage him to start early."

The foursome headed toward a bar near the far end of the room where the line was the shortest. On the way there, Ella's eyes darted from wall to wall in search of the Vincents. None of them came into view.

"So what's the game plan for tonight?" Charlotte asked. "Are we going to divide and conquer like we did at the wine tasting? Or follow the old adage *there's strength in numbers* and stick together?"

"Why don't we play it by ear?" Jake suggested. "Get a feel for the Vincents' behavior, then figure it out from there."

Miles nodded in agreement. "I like that idea. Plus, now that the town knows we've reopened Don's murder investigation, we probably need to be a bit more inconspicuous than we were at the wine tasting."

"True." Jake pointed at an empty high-top table off to the side of the main stage. "Why don't I order the drinks and you all grab some food, then snatch up that table?"

"You got it, Chief."

Miles, Charlotte and Ella headed for the buffet, filling plates with salmon tartare, steak bites, stuffed peppers and Asiago cheese. Once the foursome met back up at the table, Jake passed out the drinks and held his high in the air.

"A toast. To the four of us, getting this case solved so that we can bring justice to Don and the entire Clemmington community."

"Cheers," they exclaimed in unison.

The swing music playing in the background quieted. It was replaced by Kool & the Gang's "Celebration." The red velvet stage curtains slowly parted. When Claire, Manuel, Greer and Faith appeared, the crowd broke into applause.

Claire and Greer stepped forward first, waving while positioning themselves at the podium. Manuel and Faith came up behind them, clapping and smiling at the audience.

The sight of the family tightened Ella's throat. She swallowed the chunk of cheese she'd been chewing, quickly chasing it down with a gulp of wine.

"I wonder why Tyler and Jada aren't onstage?" Charlotte said.

Fearful of saying the wrong thing, Ella shrugged but kept her mouth closed.

Claire raised her hand to quiet the crowd. She looked radiant in a silver tuxedo dress and matching heels. Her diamond jewelry threw off laser beams each time they hit the lights, while her nude makeup showcased a smooth face that appeared freshly lifted by a plastic surgeon.

"Hello, everyone," she crooned into the mic. "Thank you very much for being here this evening. As many of you know, this particular charity event was one of Don's favorites. My husband always believed in putting education first, and that everyone should be given the opportunity to attend college. Your attendance tonight means the world to me, my family and especially the students who will have a chance to better themselves thanks to your generosity. It saddens me that Don isn't here to celebrate this joyous occasion. But he is with us in spirit. We dedicate this night to him. Thank you again for—"

A commotion erupted on the other side of the room. Heads swiveled toward the staircase that led to the second floor's high roller games. Tyler and Jada appeared at the top of the landing. He was dressed in a shiny hot pink suit. Her bandeau top and skintight miniskirt had been cut from the same cloth, literally.

"What in the…" Charlotte uttered.

Tyler pointed at the DJ and gave him a thumbs-up. Guns N' Roses' "Welcome to the Jungle" blared through the speakers. The flashy couple floated down the stairs, appearing as though they were starring in a music video rather than attending a scholarship fundraiser.

Several guests whistled and howled with glee. But the majority of the crowd looked on in shocked silence. A tap against the microphone turned everyone's attention back to the stage, where Greer stood at the podium.

"*Excuse* me, everyone," he barked. "Like my

mother was saying, we'd like to thank you for being here, and—"

"Yeah!" Tyler shouted over his brother. "Thanks for coming out, everybody!"

He and Jada strutted toward the middle of the casino. Photographers pushed their way through the crowd, falling to their knees in front of the pair while snapping away.

"This is disgusting," Ella hissed.

Once they were done with their paparazzi moment, Tyler took Jada's hand in his, twirling her around before heading to the stage.

Faith, who'd been watching it all from the sidelines, burst into tears and ran off. Claire shook her head in disdain but didn't appear as distraught as she should've. Greer continued to try to turn the crowd's attention back to them. But his chin lowered to his chest in defeat when all eyes remained on his brother and sister-in-law.

"Clemmington, Californiaaa!" Tyler yelled into the mic after shooing Greer away. "How's everybody doing tonight?"

A hesitant round of applause scattered through the crowd.

"Friends, my wife, Jada, and I could not be happier to be here. Yes, this evening is for a great cause. But it also gives us a chance to step out in our best attire, biggest jewels and fanciest cars, all while mingling with the hottest people in town. Not to mention you're sipping on *the* best wine in the country. In the *world* even. Am I right?" He leaned forward, turning his ear toward the crowd. "I said, *am I right*?"

The audience roared in agreement.

Ella grabbed her clutch, digging inside for her cell phone. "Oh, I have got to get a video of this. It is unreal."

There was another disruption near the side of the stage.

"I know, Manuel!" Claire sniffed, climbing down the stairs and rushing ahead of him. But he was hot on her sparkly kitten heels.

"*Please*, Mrs. Vincent, listen to me. You have got to do something about Tyler. The man needs to be put in check. That stunt he just pulled was beyond disrespectful!"

The pair stopped near Ella and her group's table.

"I will speak to my son when and how I see fit." She pointed at the stage, her artificially plumped lips curling into a sly smile. "You've gotta admit though, he does have that wow factor. I mean, look at the crowd. They're completely captivated!"

Manuel's eyes narrowed, his tongue clicking in rapid succession. "With all due respect, Mrs. Vincent? You're delusional."

"You may be right. But you know what else I am? *Rich.* Thanks to who? Tyler. Because ever since he took on a more prominent role, sales have skyrocketed. So if he wants to be a part of to-night's thank-you speech, who am I to stop him?"

"The owner of Vincent Vineyard, that's who. Not to mention Tyler's *mother*. The man needs to show some respect, Mrs. Vincent—"

"Are you done?" she interrupted. "Because I'm being rude. I'd like to go and greet my guests. You should too. We need to be out there personally thanking them for their support."

"One last question before you go, Mrs. Vincent. Was that Alan Monroe I saw in the crowd?"

"Yes," Claire retorted through pursed lips. "Why?"

"This may be none of my business, but don't you think having the man here who you've been accused of cheating on your husband with is a bit…*inappropriate*?"

"You're right, Manuel."

"I am?" he asked, standing a bit taller.

"Yes. You are. That *is* none of your business."

Manuel raised a hand to protest. But Claire had already sauntered off into the crowd. He just stood there, vigorously rubbing his weary red eyes.

"That poor man," Charlotte whispered. "I don't know how he can continue working for her."

"My guess is that it's his loyalty to Don," Ella responded. "But something isn't right with that woman. Her occasional grief seems forced. As if it's more for show."

"What gave it away?" Jake asked. "The fact that she's got her secret lover here, or that she allowed her crass, obnoxious son to practically take over the business?"

Miles downed the rest of his wine, then readjusted his mask. "You know, Tyler and his wife remind me of those over-the-top televangelists. They're both flamboyant, fake, attention-seeking, money hungry—"

"And most importantly," Ella interjected, "untrustworthy."

"That part," Charlotte concurred.

Through the corners of her eyes, Ella noticed Manuel drifting toward their table. They made eye contact. He stared at the group, as if trying to figure out who they were behind their masks. It didn't take long for him to recognize the officers and walk over.

"Chief Love, Detective Love, it's good to see you both here," Manuel said before nodding in Ella and Charlotte's direction. "Ladies, you both look ravishing. Thank you for coming." He didn't wait for a thank-you before turning his attention back to Jake and Miles. "Could I please talk to the two of you? Alone?"

"Of course," Jake said, setting down his glass and grabbing his phone. "We'll follow you." Before walking away, he leaned in and kissed Ella's cheek. "This should be interesting. Be right back."

The minute they were out of earshot, Charlotte grabbed her arm. "This is the best reality show I have ever seen, and it's not even being filmed! Who would've thought that a small town like Clemmington would produce such great drama?"

"Speaking of filming," Ella said, once again rummaging through her purse, "I cannot find my phone. I must've left it in the car. And I have *got* to get some footage of this fiasco before the end of the night."

"Yes, you do," Charlotte agreed. She pointed toward the stage, where Tyler and Jada were now slow dancing to the tune of UB40's "Red Red Wine" while a large crowd gathered in front, staring up at them in awe. "Apparently those two think they're celebrities, with their trashy selves. I'm being blinded by the neon pink outfits. Jada's skirt is barely covering her lady bits. And—wait, where are you going?"

"To the parking garage," Ella told her, dangling Jake's car fob in the air. "Come on. Walk with me so I can get my cell phone and—"

"*Dammit!*" Charlotte squealed.

"What's wrong?"

"Look at me," she whispered, pointing at her breasts. "I'm leaking!"

"Oh, no," Ella moaned at the sight of two stains that had seeped through her dress. "You should've worn a thicker pair of nursing pads. Did you pack extras?"

"*Extras*. How about I forgot to put any on at all! I blame it on being overly excited to get dressed up and go out. I've gotta run to the ladies room and get this situation under control."

"Do you need help?" Ella asked, following her as she shuffled toward the back of the casino.

"No, I should be fine!"

And then there was one, Ella thought. She tapped her chocolate brown manicured nails against her clutch and scanned the room. Tyler and Jada had finally left the stage. They were now lost in the crowd, along with Claire. Faith never reappeared after fleeing the stage in tears. Considering Greer was nowhere in sight, Ella assumed he was off somewhere consoling her. Being without her phone and the company she'd come with left Ella feeling alone. And vulnerable.

She eyed the entrance. People were still rolling in and out of the casino. There were guests everywhere. Her mask was securely in place, so no one would recognize her if she walked to the car alone.

You'll be fine, she told herself before heading out.

When she reached the sidewalk, Ella realized there wasn't quite as much traffic away from the casino's revolving doors. The building's bright lights grew dimmer the farther away she walked. And the parking garage seemed much closer when they'd arrived.

Just get there, get the phone and hurry back...

Ella picked up the pace, her walk turning into a slight jog as she shuffled on the balls of her feet. When she reached the garage, she flung open the glass door and pounded the elevator's up button. Several moments passed before the doors opened. A large group of people poured out, reassuring her that the lot was still bustling with activity.

"You look gorgeous!" one of the women said as she brushed past her.

"Thanks," Ella panted, rushing inside the elevator and hammering the fifth-floor button. The doors closed, but the elevator didn't move.

She laid on the button. After a few seconds, it finally began to rise. Then it stopped, dropped and stalled.

The lights flickered. Ella gripped the railing

and steadied herself, then lunged forward and hit the emergency alarm.

"How may I help you?" a perky voice chirped through the speaker.

"I'm inside the Hidden Treasure Casino's parking garage elevator, and it's stuck!"

"I am so sorry about that, ma'am. We've been having trouble with that elevator for over an hour now."

"And you didn't put up a sign? Or better yet, take it out of service?"

"We are short staffed tonight, ma'am. My apologies. I will put in a call to our service center and see how long it'll take to have someone—"

A loud beep blared through the elevator, drowning out the woman's voice. The lights went out. It took another plunge. Ella backed into a corner and screamed.

"Miss!" the operator yelled. "Are you all right?"

"No!" Ella yelled just as the elevator lit back up. It jerked once more, then rode up to the fifth floor.

The doors opened. Ella tore off her mask and sucked in a huge puff of air.

"Can you tell me exactly what's happening?"

"It looks like the elevator is working again. At least for the time being."

"Wonderful. Someone will be out there to service it as soon as possible. In the meantime, please be sure to take the stairs back down to the first floor."

"Of course," Ella wheezed, stumbling out of the vestibule and into the lot.

Rows and rows of cars blended together. She squinted, peering into the dimly lit distance in search of Jake's.

Per usual, she hadn't paid attention to where they'd parked. Ella struck the alarm fob over and over, waiting to hear a beep or see blinking tail-lights. Only dark silence filled the air.

The eerie clicking of her heels against the cement echoed off the walls. She darted down one row and up another, still gasping from the panic of being stuck in the confines of a malfunctioning elevator.

Ominous shadows appeared in her peripheral. When she moved, they moved. She stopped, pressing her body against a nearby pillar. And then it dawned on her. The shadows were a reflection of her own body, rushing past the shiny cars' exteriors.

Ella closed her eyes and drew in a deep breath. *Your mind is playing tricks on you. Calm down. Find the car. And get back to the casino.*

She stepped away from the column and set

off toward the second to last row of cars. Hit the alarm fob again.

Bloop, bloop.

"Thank you!" she shrieked as lights blinked up ahead.

Running at full speed, she somehow managed not to twist her ankle while charging toward the car.

Ella threw open the door. The phone wasn't on the passenger seat. She felt around on the floor until her hand landed on it.

Dread slithered across her skin as she closed the door. Now she had to find her way back to the first floor. Alone. Through the stairwell.

Call Jake. Have him meet you here while you wait inside the car.

Her fingers quivered as she dialed his number. "Please answer…"

Ella held the phone to her ear, anxious to hear his voice. The other end of the line was silent. Several moments passed before three beeps pinged in her ear. She glared at the screen.

Call failed.

No reception.

"Dammit!"

Ella spun around, wishing that a security guard would suddenly appear. No such luck. An exit sign blinked in the far right corner. She set off toward it, willing her aching calves to get her there.

"Hey!" someone barked.

Ella stopped. Pivoted. No one appeared.

A sickening chill settled in her chest.

Keep going!

She charged toward the exit sign, sprinting through the middle of the aisle.

"Hey, you!" the commanding voice called out. "In the burgundy dress. Stop!"

A shadowy figure emerged from behind a purple pickup truck. Ella prayed that it was a guest of the charity event, and a plus-one would appear. But the person was alone.

Stop looking over your shoulder. Turn around and get to the stairwell!

Footsteps pounded behind her. The faster she ran, the closer they got.

Ella reached the corridor. Grabbed the handle and ripped open the door. Ran down the stairs as if her stilettos were sneakers, gripping the banister while taking them two at a time. She jumped when the door slammed behind her, then winced at the creaking sound of it reopening.

"You thought that mask was gonna hide your identity?" someone yelled from above. "I recognized you the minute you strolled through the door!"

"Leave me alone!" Ella screamed.

"Oh, I will. Once you get the hell out of Clemmington!"

This is a nightmare. I never should've come here. I knew better! I have got to talk to Jake…

Tears streamed down her face. The stairs grew distorted, transforming into what appeared to be gray slopes of dirt. Ella kept going, determined to escape the garage alive.

Her aching feet weakened. The straps on her shoes sliced into her skin. She ignored the pain after seeing that she'd reached level two.

Almost there. Keep going. Faster!

Ella's assailant appeared at the top of the landing. He was getting closer. So was the exit. She sped up until finally, the first floor exit appeared.

"Yes!" she screamed, throwing open the door.

Boom!

Ella slammed into someone standing on the other side. She cried out. How in hell did the attacker beat her there?

The man gripped her arms as she tried to fight him off, then held her upright before she went crumbling to the ground.

"El!" he yelled. "What is going on?"

She froze. Looked up at the man. It was Jake.

Ella grabbed hold of him, then turned to see if her attacker was still in the stairwell. He was gone.

Pull yourself together. Now!

"I… I just got turned around in the lot," she said, straightening her dress. "Then the elevator malfunctioned, and I had to take the stairs back down."

"Okay, well, Charlotte told me you'd come to the car to get your phone. She thought you would've made it back to the casino by now. So I came to check on you."

Thank God…

"Are you okay?"

"Yeah," Ella lied. "I'm fine."

Jake kept an arm wrapped firmly around her shoulders on the way back to the casino. "I've got to catch you up on what happened when Miles and I spoke with Manuel. That Tyler… He is something else."

"Can't wait to hear all about it," Ella mumbled, wondering when she'd get up the nerve to tell Jake the truth.

Chapter Eight

Jake and Miles sat across from one another inside the police station's conference room, waiting on Greer to arrive. They'd opted to meet with him there instead of the vineyard so that he could speak freely.

"Let's not rule Greer out as a possible suspect just because his mother and brother appear to have a stronger motive," Jake warned.

"Oh, I'm not ruling anybody out. The Vincents are one strange family. I can't wait to hear what the brothers' wives have to say about all this too."

"My guess is that Tyler's wife will ride for him until the end. Her loyalty seems obsessive, almost cultlike."

"I couldn't agree more," Miles said. "Those two are the perfect match. Like the male and female version of one another. But both wives have one goal in mind, and that is to see their husbands take over as president of Vincent Vineyard."

"To the point where one of them may have been complicit in having Don killed. And not to take the focus off of those two, but do you have an update on the men who broke into the vineyard's offices during that tour?"

"I've put in calls to Mitch and Dylan letting them know we need to speak with them as soon as possible. Still waiting on callbacks. As for that wild one, Ben Foray, I'm having trouble locating him. San Diego PD is helping to track him down since that was his last known place of residence."

Jake tapped his pen against the table, staring at his most recent case notes. "Good. I wish we could've gotten more information out of Manuel at the charity event. But are we surprised that Tyler ran over and interrupted us before the conversation even got started?"

"I certainly wasn't."

"Tyler knows that Manuel holds the key to helping us solve Don's murder. He also knew that Manuel was heated after the stunt he and Jada pulled at the charity event. He made his presence known as an intimidation tactic, just to keep Manuel quiet."

Miles tore open a packet of sugar and poured it inside his World's Best Dad mug of coffee.

"And it worked. You see Manuel didn't utter a word about the case after Tyler walked up. Wouldn't it be something if Claire and Tyler were in on all this together, and they conspired to kill Don?"

"It would be. From what I'm seeing, I wouldn't rule that theory out either."

A text message notification from Ella popped up on Jake's buzzing phone.

Hey babe. Hope your day is going well. Charlotte and I are going to grab lunch. I'll wait at her place until you get off work. Can you pick me up from there? XO

Of course, love. Enjoy. See you tonight.

"Judging by that goofy grin on your face," Miles snarked, "I'm guessing that's Ella texting you?"

"You've got a lot of nerve given the way you giggle like a clown every time Charlotte looks your way."

Miles balled up a napkin and threw it in Jake's direction. "Dude, I was only kidding. No need to take low blows!"

Jake caught the napkin right before it hit his forehead, then glanced at the time. Greer was almost thirty minutes late. "I wonder what's taking our guy so long to get here. I hope Tyler didn't find out he was coming in and pull something to deter him."

"I wouldn't put it past him." Miles paused, taking a long sip of coffee. "Hey, what was going on with Ella the night of the charity event? It seemed like after you two came back from the parking garage, she was shaken up."

"Ugh," Jake groaned, running his hand along the back of his neck. "I don't know, man. Your guess is as good as mine. When I got to the garage, I saw that the elevator wasn't working. So I went to the stairwell, and the second I opened the door, *bam!* Ella came flying through the doorway and fell into my arms. She seemed completely disoriented."

"Do you think something happen to her inside the garage?"

"I have no clue. She said she'd gotten stuck in the elevator on her way up to the car, then got freaked out by the dark creepy stairwell on the way back down. The more questions I asked, the more she shut down. So I just left it alone. It was definitely weird though."

"Hmm. Well, after that attack in the corn maze and, of course, Ella's ex-boyfriend being the Numeric Serial Killer, we shouldn't be surprised."

Jake propped his elbows on the table and rubbed his hands together. "Yeah... I've tried talking her into getting therapy, but so far, she's refused. Adamantly."

"Really? I'm surprised. Especially considering she's a nurse. After everything she has been through, you would think she'd understand how much counseling would benefit her."

There was a knock at the door.

"*Finally,*" Jake muttered before calling out, "come in!"

Lena cracked open the door and stuck her head inside. "Hey, sorry to interrupt. No Greer yet?"

"Nope." Miles checked his phone. "Not yet. No call or text saying he'd be late either."

"I'll text him now to find out his ETA," Jake said. "Let's just hope Tyler didn't get inside his head and convince him not to come."

Lena moved farther inside the doorway, balancing a box with a stack of files on top.

"What's all that?" Miles asked.

"I finally found the evidence from Don's crime scene that we couldn't locate. It was in the back of the storage closet Dad used as his personal property room. I think he'd stored it there for safekeeping, just to make sure it didn't get misplaced."

"Did you find anything worth being retested?" Jake asked.

"I did. Don's clothes are here, samples of the soil surrounding the area where his body was found, a pair of thinning shears and a serrated grape knife."

"*Wait*!" Jake jumped up and peering inside the box. "You said you've got a grape knife?"

"I did. Why?"

"I was just wondering if that could be the—"

"Murder weapon?" Lena interrupted. "I'm way ahead of you."

The conversation pulled Miles from his chair. He walked over, his lips twisted with skepticism. "Hold on. If that was the weapon used to kill Don, don't you think the Definitive Solutions Crime Lab would've discovered that through DNA testing?"

"Possibly," Lena replied. "But it won't hurt for me to run it again and see what I may find since our lab's technology is more advanced than theirs."

"I agree," Jake said. "Let us know if something comes of it."

As Lena turned to walk out, she was stopped by Lucy, the police station's administrative assistant.

"Oops, sorry," Lucy said, quickly stepping aside. "Chief Love, Detective Love, I've got Greer Vincent here to see you."

"Thanks, Lucy," Jake replied, watching as Greer peered inside the room. "Come on in, Mr. Vincent. Have a seat."

Greer shuffled through the door with his head hanging low. His dull skin appeared ashen. Dark bags cradled his puffy eyes. A scruffy beard covered his haggard face, and he appeared about three weeks overdue for a haircut.

"*This should be good,*" Lena whispered to Jake before closing the door behind her.

He took a seat at the head of the table. "Thank you for coming in to speak with us, Mr. Vincent. And congratulations on such a successful charity event. I'm sure it'll help a lot of students attend college this year."

Greer snorted loudly, wringing his hands while staring down at the table. "Yeah. Thanks. But I really don't wanna talk about the charity event. You guys called me down here. What can I do for you?"

His flat tone reeked of defeat. Jake pitied him, almost feeling bad for having to question him.

Ignore it. Press on. Find out what he has to say.

"As you know, Clemmington PD has reopened your father's death investigation. We are determined to make an arrest this go-round, and we're hoping you'd be willing to share your thoughts on what was going on around the time of his murder."

An awkward silence filled the room. Greer had yet to make eye contact with Jake or Miles.

"Mr. Vincent," Miles said, "are you all right? Can I get you anything to—"

"Mr. Vincent was my father' name. Please, call me Greer. And no, I don't need anything. I'm fine." He finally looked up and glared at Jake. "What exactly are you going to do differently to find the killer this time? Your dad's investigation came up empty, despite him having years of experience. Better yet, is this really about you bringing justice to my family? Or are you trying to prove that you actually earned the position of police chief? Because rumor has it you bypassed a few more qualified candidates thanks to a little thing called nepotism."

Jake's eyes narrowed as he stared back at Greer. The urge to bite back simmered on his tongue. He bit down on his cheek, refusing to stoop to Greer's level, while flipping open his notebook. "Mr. Vin—my apologies, *Greer*, in your opinion, what was life like for your father around the time of his death? Were things normal? Did he seem down, feel threatened or experience any sort of strange run-in with someone?"

A guttural moan bellowed from Greer's wide open mouth. "I can't do this!" he wailed before bursting into tears.

Miles jumped up and handed him a box of tissues. The unexpected outburst transformed Jake's irritation into concern. When Greer's head hit the mahogany tabletop, the chief placed a hand on his shoulder.

"I cannot believe this has happened to my family," Greer moaned. "Who would've done this? *Why* would someone have done this?"

"That's what we're working hard on to figure out," Jake assured him. "My sister, Lena, who's an expert forensic scientist, is retesting crime scene evidence inside our new state-of-art lab as we speak."

After Greer failed to raise his head, Miles chimed in. "We're also going to be bringing persons of interest back in for questioning and running polygraph tests. Including the men who broke into your father's office during that tour of the vineyard."

Those words pulled Greer up from the table. "Good," he croaked before wiping his face with a tissue before blowing his nose into it. "I was always suspicious of those jackasses. But your father didn't seem to think they were viable suspects. He was set on the idea of my dad's murder being an inside job. Meaning someone in the family committed it."

Jake propped his chin in his hand, slowly nodding. "Well, I'm leaning into that theory as well. If Mr. Vincent's murder was in fact an inside job, who do you think would've done it?"

An obnoxious laugh crept through Greer's

sniffles. "Listen, I hate to throw my own brother under the bus, but Tyler is the only answer. He's the one who'd have the most to gain."

"I hope this doesn't come across as disrespectful," Miles interjected, "but what about your mother?"

"She obviously had something to gain as well."

Jake's neck swiveled at his candidness. But he kept his cool to keep Greer talking. "Do you think it's a possibility that they both had something to do with the murder?"

Several seconds passed before Greer replied, "To be honest, I don't think my mother was involved. She had it made, whether my father was dead or alive. The big house, the fancy cars, the designer clothes and expensive jewelry, not to mention the status of saying she's Vincent Vineyard's COO. My mom even had a lover on the side—"

"Hold on," Miles interrupted while rigorously taking notes. "Your mother's affair was public knowledge?"

"I mean, yes and no. Was it discussed out in the open? No, not really. But did people around town whisper about it behind closed doors? Absolutely. The worst part was that Alan Monroe and my father had been rivals for years. My mom knew that. Of all the men she could've been with, she chose him." Greer hesitated as a few lone tears trickled down his face. "My father did mention divorce a few times, but my mother knew he'd never leave her. So she never took him seriously."

"What are you saying?" Jake asked. "Mrs. Vincent didn't have a strong enough motive to kill your father?"

"In my opinion? No."

"Okay then. Let's get back to Tyler."

A cluster of angry lines formed between Greer's eyebrows. "What about him?"

"You said he'd have the strongest motive. Tell us why."

"Weren't you two at the wine tasting? You saw the man make a complete fool of himself in front of the entire crowd, as if he knows anything about…about *wine*, and…and *harvesting*, and business in general. All the man knows is flamboyance. And attention. Putting on for the cameras. He wants the power. He wants to be the king of Vincent Vineyard. But the problem is, Tyler doesn't possess the knowledge or skill set to do so. What he does possess, however, is the ability to charm the hell out of my mother. And our employees. The patrons. The whole damn community, really."

Greer paused, gulping down a bottle of water until there was none left. He jumped from his chair and grabbed another off the shelf, then began pacing the floor.

"And don't even get me started on Tyler's

wife. Jada is just as bad as he is, if not worse. I'm talking money hungry, power hungry, superficial, cold… I could go on about her all day. What I can't understand is how my wife can tolerate her. They are *complete* opposites."

"Aside from the fact that they're sisters-in-law," Miles said, "does your wife have a significant relationship with Jada outside of the vineyard, or would you consider them to be more like work friends?"

Greer plopped back down into his chair and stared up at the ceiling. "Oh, they definitely have a significant relationship outside of the vineyard. For some odd reason, Faith considers Jada to be one of her closest friends. And all Jada does is take advantage of her. Dumps her work off on Faith. Even forced my wife to take computer courses so she could serve as the vineyard's tech expert after Tyler refused to pay for a consultant. Faith took on all that responsibility with no additional pay too."

"Understood. But that's work-related. What is their personal relationship like?"

"*Tuh*," Greer sputtered, his lips forming a sour pucker. "It's one-sided, to say the least. Whenever Tyler does something to upset Jada, she comes running to Faith. And Faith is always there to console her. Then Tyler buys Jada some expensive apology gift, and she goes right back to being happy again. Then he messes up once more and she comes running back to Faith, and the cycle continues. All Jada cares about is Tyler, and all Tyler cares about is Tyler. In the meantime, maintaining Vincent Vineyard is left up to my wife, Manuel and, of course, me."

The defeated look in Greer's eyes weighed heavily on Jake. He knew how close Greer was to his father. To have endured that loss, then deal with a mother, brother and sister-in-law who didn't seem to care had to be excruciating.

"I know this is tough on you, Greer," the chief said. "You have my condolences."

"Mine as well," Miles added quietly.

"Thank you. I appreciate that. And uh…sorry about the outburst—"

Jake held his hand in the air. "Please. Don't apologize. Believe me, we understand. You've been through a lot. I appreciate your raw honesty. And your transparency. You have no idea how many people come in here with a stoic, emotionless wall up. It's as if they don't want to show any sign of humanity for fear of appearing guilty, even when they're not. So we appreciate your candidness."

"I hope at least some of what I shared gave you a little more insight into the vineyard's dynamics."

"It definitely did." Jake cleared his throat, tapping his pen against his palm. "Greer, where were you at the time of your father's murder?"

"I was inside the distillery, overseeing new equipment installation."

Just as Tyler said.

"Okay then," Jake replied. "I guess we can wrap this up…" He hesitated when Greer slid away from the table, sitting up straighter and crossing one leg over the other.

"You know, Chief Love, there is something else weighing heavily on me that I feel compelled to share. If I may."

"Of course. Please do."

"I don't want either of you to be totally fooled by my brother's antics. Tyler may be a clown, but when it comes to doing what's best for Vincent Vineyard? He's all in. I mean, is he the sharpest knife in the drawer? Obviously not. Husband of the year? Never. Do we have our fair share of disagreements? Absolutely. But I blame that on our big brother-little brother dynamic, you know what I mean? I'm sure you both do, considering you're brothers and all, right?"

Jake glanced at Miles, whose expression was just as perplexed as his. "I'm sorry, Greer, but where are you going with all this?"

"Okay, let me break it down in a way that'll be as palatable as possible. Since my father's death, running Vincent Vineyard has been so much easier. I'm talking more pleasant. More productive. More profitable. More…more *everything*. We no longer have to beg, and overexplain and kiss anybody's ass to get what we want. If I pitch an idea that'll enhance the business and increase our profit margin, I get an immediate yes. Oh, and just between us, I talked Tyler into secretly planting several new grape varieties in the vineyard a few years ago, after my father refused to expand the wine selection."

A loud silence filled the room.

Tread carefully, Jake thought, his mind racing with confusion. *This might be the new intel you've been looking for…*

"How did you manage to pull that off behind your father's back? Didn't he keep a close eye on those fields?"

"He did. But I worked around it. I knew Tyler had a ton of extra cash at his disposal, so I convinced him to pay the vine workers hush money to make it happen. They worked late at night, long after my father had gone home. It's a shame how the grapes were ready to be harvested right before his death. He never got a chance to see how profitable the new lines of wine have been."

A sick feeling settled in the pit of Jake's gut. Greer's shift in demeanor was alarming, as was his admission and love/hate relationship with his brother. But none of that was enough to charge him with a crime.

"What did your mother have to say once she found out about all this?" Miles asked.

"Found out? She was in on it from the very beginning. Unlike my father, Claire is extremely business-minded. She didn't give a damn about Don's traditions and old-school way of doing things. She's all about making a profit. Period."

"Did Manuel know about these secret grape varieties that you planted?"

"Of course not. Manuel was way too loyal to my father. Had he known, he would've gone straight to Don and snitched. And then, who knows what would've happened." Greer glanced casually at his watch. "On that note, I need to get out of here. I'm meeting with a wine distributor, and I can't be late. God forbid I let Tyler run it on his own. He'd ruin the sale before it even closed with all his boasting and false promises. Yet *another* reason I should've been named president a long time ago…"

His words felt all too familiar. They were the exact ones Tyler had spoken about him. After his declaration, Greer appeared just as ruthless as his brother.

Maybe he isn't the good stand-up guy he'd portrayed himself to be…

Greer stood, stretching as if he'd just awakened from a long peaceful nap, then headed for the door. "Thanks again for the vent session, officers. Enjoy the rest of your day."

And with that, he walked out.

Jake and Miles peered at the door, then one another, their expressions frozen in shock. Several moments passed before Miles spoke up.

"First of all, what in the hell was *that*? This interview took a turn that I did not see coming. Secondly, how many different personalities did we just witness in one man?"

"I lost count. I think it's safe to say that Greer has completely lost the plot. We have got to get Manuel in here as soon as possible. He's the one who'll give us some real insight into this entire situation."

"Haven't you reached out to him?"

Jake sat back, sliding his notebook aside in frustration. "I have. He keeps claiming to be too busy to get down here. I think he's afraid of saying something that might incriminate Claire since his loyalty now lies with her."

"Well, if he can't come to us, then we need to go to him."

"Don't worry. I'll get him in here. In the meantime, I'm adding Greer's name to our list of suspects, right next to Tyler's."

Chapter Nine

Ella sat in front of her laptop, eyeing the woman staring back at her through the screen. She had a youthful air despite being well over sixty. Her long fluffy blond hair cascaded down the sides of her pleasant face, outlining dimpled cheeks and a genial smile. The woman's gentle tone and calming demeanor put Ella at ease, enabling her to open up in ways she'd never expected.

"So, Ella, tell me. Why haven't you shared the fact that you're undergoing therapy with Jake?"

Peering blankly at the keyboard, Ella's mind swirled for a response. Telling Jake would mean delving into what she'd been hiding. She still wasn't ready to reveal her secret to him nor to her therapist. All Ella really wanted was help getting through the trauma of her past, and ways to cope with the attacks she'd recently experienced.

"I don't know, Mrs. Lane. Jake is going through so much right now, with this investigation and all the scrutiny. I don't think he realized how challenging reopening this case would be. Now that the cat's out the bag, Clemmington is expecting an arrest. Immediately. That, plus being the new chief of police, is a heavy burden to carry. So to answer your question, I don't want to give him another thing to worry about."

"The fact that you're in therapy is a good thing, Ella. Not a worry. You're Jake's partner. He loves you. He wants you to heal from all that you've been through. Just like his investigation, you are a high priority as well, just a different kind. Plus, isn't Jake the one who recommended that you seek counseling? That alone tells me that he cares. I can't tell you how many of my clients have sought therapy against their partners' will."

Ella pressed her hands against the sides of her face, ruminating on her words.

She doesn't get it. No one does. Because they don't know the truth...

"Listen," Mrs. Lane continued, "I understand the toll that the attacks have taken on you. We're working through that. But this secret that's haunting you, that you're afraid to share with anyone, do you understand that until *I* know what it is, I cannot help you through it?"

Ella nodded, remaining silent for fear that if she opened her mouth to speak, a sob would come rolling out. When Mrs. Lane sat quietly, awaiting a response, Ella finally whispered, "I'm just not ready to talk about it. I'll open up eventually, but not right now."

"I understand. Well, whenever you're ready, I'll be here. In the meantime, have you worked on any of those coping tactics that we discussed during your last session to help manage the anxiety?"

Sliding her notebook toward her, Ella flipped to the page where she'd written a list of strategies. "I have. I've been taking some time to meditate first thing in the morning and throughout the day whenever I start feeling uneasy. And I'm writing in my journal again, allowing myself to feel whatever emotions I'm dealing with from day to day. If I'm sad, I face the sadness. If I wanna cry, I let it out."

Mrs. Lane broke into applause. "I'm loving the progress, Ella. When I first suggested you begin journaling, you were very much against it. But look at you now. Great work. Do you notice a difference in how you're processing your emotions?"

"I do. I've just been letting them flow, which has enabled me to let them go. Well...not *completely*. But I'm getting there."

After checking her clock, the therapist clasped her hands together. "Some progress is better than no progress at all, my dear. Now, it looks like we're almost out of time. Is there anything else you'd like to share with me, or that you'll be focusing on during this upcoming week?"

"Yes, there is. I've been reading up on how diet and exercise can help reduce stress. Of course I'm aware of that considering I'm a nurse. But I hadn't ever really considered eating in moderation and working out on a regular basis. So I've incorporated those two things into my daily routine, and I'm already seeing a difference in my mental state. I'm thinking more clearly and remaining calmer when issues arise that would normally get me riled up."

"That's wonderful, Ella. A heathy diet and consistent exercise routine can absolutely help curb your stress and anxiety. Speaking of which, what about the work you've been doing to assist in the investigation? Have you discussed with Jake the need to pull back on your involvement since it may be triggering your anxiety?"

Ella bit down on her lip, resisting the urge to lie. She had yet to tell Jake that she needed time away from the case for the sake of her mental health. As far as she was concerned, it wasn't an issue. But her therapist thought otherwise.

While the investigation was interesting and keeping her busy throughout the day, deep down, Ella knew that there could be some truth to Mrs. Lane's suggestion. Maybe pulling back would be a good thing. Because the case was a constant reminder of her ties to the Vincent family, the attacks she'd endured and the fact that someone wanted her dead.

The buzz of Mrs. Lane's alarm rattled the speakers, jolting Ella from her thoughts.

"That's our time, Ella. We can pick up right where we left off next week. Are you still able to keep your standing appointment?"

"I am, thank you. Looking forward to it." Her hand hovered over the top of the computer screen. "See you then—" Ella paused at the sound of sleigh bells jingling outside of the loft.

"Good to see you too, Mr. Stevenson," someone said on the other side of the front door.

Jake.

When the jingling grew louder, Ella realized they weren't sleigh bells. They were his keys, sliding inside the door.

Mrs. Lane threw a finger in the air. "Oh, wait! One more thing. Don't forget to check your email for this week's homework assignment."

Ella pounded the volume button on the laptop until it was practically silent. "Will do," she uttered, her eyes peeled to the doorway.

"I think this assignment will be particularly helpful in reducing your stress levels. It's a visualization exercise that follows the mind-over-matter mantra. The way it works is, when you think of those moments you were attacked in the corn maze, chased through the park, stalked inside the parking garage or received threatening messages, you detach yourself from them. Immediately. And replace them with a visual that's peaceful and safe. Put yourself in a place where you feel calm. And relaxed. What does that look like to you? Is it a sunny beach? A mountainside cabin? A stunning ski slope—"

"*Mrs. Lane,*" Ella interrupted just as the door opened, "is all this information included in your email?"

"Yes, it is. And thank you for stopping me. I was on a roll and just realized my next patient is waiting in the queue. I'll send the assignment over as soon as I'm done with—"

"That sounds great. Thanks again for today!"

Ella slammed the laptop shut and scurried into the living room. "Hey, babe! How was your day?"

"Hey." Jake sighed, giving her a kiss so quick that it barely grazed her lips. "My day was unreal, to put it lightly. Greer came in and spoke to Miles and me. You would not believe some of the things that man said to us. Let's just say he is not who we thought he was. That whole mister meek-and-humble act? It's just that. An act." He paused, leaning his head back and pulling in a sharp breath of air. "What is that deliciousness I smell?"

"Blackened chicken."

"Mmm," Jake moaned, following Ella into the kitchen. "That sounds good. What is it with you and all this cooking? You trying to spoil me into putting a ring on it?"

She waved her left hand in the air. "Maybe… But seriously, I'm just trying to keep us fit and healthy."

"Okay, I can respect that. What are we having to go along with the chicken?"

"A Cobb salad. We've got a mix of baby spinach and chopped romaine, hard boiled eggs, cherry tomatoes, cucumbers, red onions, a little blue cheese and a red wine vinaigrette."

Jake leaned against the counter, watching her intently. The soft smile on his face crinkled the corners of his deep-set eyes. The loving expression caused a tinge of guilt to singe her chest.

You'll tell him everything eventually. Just not today.

"I love that we're having a nice salad as a starter," he continued, popping a tomato inside his mouth. "I need more veggies in my life. What side dishes did you whip up?"

"No side dishes. Just the Cobb salad topped with the chicken. Oh! And garlic-flavored protein croutons too."

"What are you trying to do to me, woman? Starve me or something? Can we at least throw in a little mac and cheese or sweet potato fries, some creamy risotto… Hell, *anything* to go along with it!"

"Says Clemmington's new chief of police who needs to be in great shape in order to run down all those criminals," Ella reminded him while pulling down a couple of salad bowls.

"Yeah, okay. Don't be mad if I pop a frozen pizza in the oven later tonight."

"You'd better not!" She bumped her hip against his side as he washed up at the sink, jumping when his cell phone vibrated against her thigh.

He dried his hands and checked the notification. "*Yes*, finally!"

"Good news?"

"Great news. Manuel is ready to come into the station and talk with me. Judging by the tone of this text, he sounds determined this time."

Leaning over his shoulder, Ella peered at the screen and scanned the message. "That is awesome. But wait, what is that he's saying about Greer?"

"Oh, *wow*. So apparently, when Greer left the police station today and returned to the vineyard, Manuel overheard him talking to his wife. Greer told Faith that he'd accomplished his goal of throwing off law enforcement by sprinkling bits of incriminating evidence over everyone close to Don's murder investigation."

"What? Why would he do something like that?"

Hunching his shoulders, Jake scanned the message once again. "I have no idea. You know, he was acting really weird when we questioned him. But it never dawned on me that he was scheming on us. How sad is it that Don's own son would rather play games than bring justice to his killer?"

"Maybe because Greer *is* the killer. Either way, it's disgusting. Don deserves better than this. From what you've told me, he was an upstanding man who was good to his entire family. And what do they do? Push him out to gain control of the business that *he* built. I swear, the Vincents take the phrase *money is the root of all evil* to another level."

"Hold on," Jake interjected as he continued scrolling through the text. "Listen to this. Manuel also overheard Faith tell Greer that he should've pointed the finger directly at the person he thought committed the murder, even if it is his own mother."

The serving spoon fell from Ella's hand. "So what is she saying? That Greer thinks Claire killed Don?"

"That's what it sounds like to me."

As Jake began replying to the message, Ella's mind shifted. Visions of being chased inside that dark dank parking garage stairwell appeared.

She squeezed her eyes shut, her therapist's words popping into her head.

Detach yourself. Immediately.

Thoughts of a warm serene beachside drowned out the noise. She walked along the soft sand, its grainy surface massaging the soles of her bare feet. Ella felt safe, calm, at peace...

"...and I cannot *wait* to hear what he has to say for himself," Jake barked, grabbing the serving spoon and filling their bowls with chicken and salad.

"Wait, I'm sorry. I must've zoned out. You can't wait to hear what who has to say for himself?"

"Ben Foray. Please don't tell me you missed my entire rant."

Ella turned her head, avoiding Jake's curious gaze as she poured two glasses of Riesling. "I believe I did. Sorry, babe. Run it by me again, please?"

"I was saying that Miles received a call from Mitch Wilkerson? Remember him? Ben's friend who broke into Don's office with him?"

"I do. What did he have to say for himself?"

"He's agreed to talk to us. *And*, he confided

that Ben isn't in San Diego. He's been hiding out at Mitch's place right here in Clemmington for the past few weeks. Mitch thinks he may try and leave town soon, so we need to catch up with him before that happens."

"That's awesome, babe," Ella said as they sat down at the table. "Despite Greer's strange behavior, you all are making great progress."

"We are. Once I speak with Manuel, things should really start coming together. At least that's my hope."

"Mine too. He's got to be fed up. And things around the vineyard are only going to get more hectic now that the one-year anniversary of Don's death is upon us. It's finally time to name one of the Vincent sons president."

Jake's unblinking eyes stared into his glass as he twirled the stem between his fingertips. "Let's just pray that Manuel doesn't let us down. Because like I told Miles, he holds the key that'll crack this case wide open."

Chapter Ten

Jake pulled open the Hole in the Wall dive bar's flimsy wooden door. Before stepping inside, the stench of mold, cigarettes and marijuana smacked him in the face.

"*Damn*," Miles grunted, waving his hand in front of his nose. "This place is foul."

"And that's putting it nicely."

Clouds of smoke lingered over the trucker hat-covered heads crowding the bar. Country music blared from a run-down jukebox propped in the corner. A group of men were in the throes of a heated pool game near the back. Mugs of beer were being tossed back faster than they could be poured.

It wasn't an ideal location to question Mitch and Ben. But Mitch had tipped Jake off earlier that day, letting him know they'd be there that night. Since Jake wanted to confront Ben before he skipped town, he didn't have much choice.

"Why does it seem like this establishment just popped out of nowhere?" Miles yelled.

"Well, for starters, we're never on this side of town. And when I looked it up online, I found out it had been closed for a while after getting shut down for failing the food health inspection."

"I am not the least bit surprised by that," Miles quipped as he and Jake made their way farther inside.

The rickety wooden tables lining the narrow bar's outdated paneling were packed, making it difficult for the officers to squeeze through the crowd.

"Did Mitch say exactly where he and Ben would be sitting?"

"Far right corner in the back, over by the kitchen."

"I cannot believe they actually serve food here," Miles said as buckets of hot wings filled practically every table.

Holding in a fit of coughs, Jake peered through the haze. He spotted two men hunched over a lopsided pub table, clearly not wanting to be seen. One of them had a blond buzz cut. The other had his long brown hair pulled into a ponytail and a pair of sunglasses propped on top of his head.

"I think I've spotted our guys," Jake told Miles.

"Lead the way."

The chief casually approached the table, tapping Mitch's shoulder and extending his hand. He'd already informed Mitch that they would be keeping things cool so as not to appear suspicious and alarm Ben.

"What's up, Mitch?"

"Hey, how's it going, Chief Love?"

"*Chief*," Ben slurred, attempting to jump up from his stool but instead falling against the wall. "Chief of *what*?"

"Chief of police. Clemmington's to be exact," he replied, grabbing Ben's arm and helping him back onto his stool. "I'm Jake Love. This is my brother, Detective Miles Love."

Ben ignored Jake's extended hand, glaring across the table at Mitch through bloodshot eyes. "What the hell is this about, man? You setting me up or something?"

"*What*? No! Of course not. I didn't even know these guys were gonna be here."

"Sure you didn't. Damn snitch…"

"Listen," Miles interjected. "Chief Love and I just so happened to be in the area, we're off the clock, and wanted to stop in and grab a couple of beers. Speaking of which, can we buy you two another round?"

Ben snatched up his cell phone and began typing away. "Nope. I'm good. A drink coming from you might be spiked with pig's blood."

Just get down to business, Jake thought, realizing the niceties weren't going to work.

"In case you two hadn't heard," he said, "Clemmington PD has reopened Don Vincent's murder investigation. You're familiar with the case, aren't you?"

Mitch's eyes darted from the officers to Ben, who remained silent while staring down at his phone. "Um…yeah, we're familiar. I'm surprised you all never caught the guy who did it."

"So are we. Mr. Vincent was killed a few days after you two were at the vineyard. On that group tour—"

"*And*?" Ben interrupted, glaring up at Jake. "So what?"

"We reviewed some interesting surveillance footage from that day. You two, along with your friend Dylan, were caught breaking into Mr. Vincent's office. Ben, I believe it was you who left there with an envelope that fell from your pocket. Would you mind telling us what was inside of it?"

Ben snatched up his mug and drained it, then discharged a smelly burp. "Yeah, I do mind. Now what?"

Miles moved closer to Ben and leaned into his ear. "We could always take this conversation down to the police station and have it there, if you think you'd be more comfortable inside an interrogation room. It's up to you."

Suddenly Ben sat straight up, nodding while wiping his eyes. "Nah, I think I'm good here. I do remember being at the vineyard that day. But what I *don't* remember is breaking into some office. Actually, you know what happened? My buddy Mitch here escorted me to a private area, and I just followed his lead, thinking it was all a part of the tour."

The group turned to Mitch. His crooked jaw hung open, but he didn't utter a word.

"*Right*, Mitch?" Ben spat through clenched coffee-stained teeth. When he failed to get a response, Ben pointed at Jake. "Look, what is this really about, man? Back when everything went down at the vineyard, the police showed up and questioned us. Then nothing came of it and we were sent on our way. The owner didn't bother to press charges. So why are you heckling me about it a year later?"

"Because, once again, shortly after that incident, Mr. Vincent turned up stabbed to death in the middle of the grape fields. Which is mighty suspicious, considering you fought with him days prior to the murder—"

Bzzzz...

Ben's cell phone vibrated so forcefully that it almost skidded off the table. Jake caught a glimpse of the screen right before Ben grabbed it. The name that appeared almost knocked him to the sawdust-covered floor.

Jada Vincent.

"What's up, babe?" Ben yelled into the phone. "No, I told you to *text* me back, not call. Why? What do you mean why? Because it's…it's hot in here! Get it? *Really* hot!"

Miles turned his head away from the group and leaned toward Jake. "You know that comment wasn't about the bar's steamy temperature, right?"

"Of course. It was all about us. And you'll never guess who he's talking to."

When Ben shot him a look, Jake pulled out his cell phone and texted Miles.

That's Jada Vincent on the other end of the line!

Miles's shoulders slowly caved as he read the message. He nodded discreetly, replying, We'll get to the bottom of that in due time. For now, let's just stick to the script.

"I don't know if they will!" Ben continued to rant. "But just in case they do, alert my law— my *guy* so that he'll be on call." After a few moments of silence, he yelled out, "No! *Blackman*."

In his drunken state, Ben failed to realize the overtness of his thinly veiled code words. Blackman & Associates was one of the largest and most well-respected law firms in the area.

"Look, I gotta go," Ben continued. "Yeah, yeah, I'll let you know. Just make sure you hold up *your* end of the bargain."

He slammed the phone against the table and grabbed Mitch's drink, gulping it down in two swallows. Mitch just sat there, slouching in defeat.

"You done with your call?" Jake asked. "Maybe I can proceed with what I was saying?"

"Sure, Chief. You may proceed."

"So, what was inside that envelope you stole from Don Vincent's office?"

Ben's phone buzzed again. Charles Blackman's name appeared on the screen, owner of Blackman & Associates.

"Sorry, gents," Ben said, hopping up so quickly that he stumbled backward. Jake grabbed hold of him right before he fell against a dart board hanging from the wall. He stood and shook it off, then staggered toward the kitchen. "I gotta take this. Mitch, do a little strip tease or something to keep these guys entertained until I get back. *If* I come back."

The moment Ben was out of earshot, Mitch turned to the officers. "Chief Love, Detective Love, I am so sorry about this. I knew Ben wouldn't be an easy nut to crack, but I had no idea he'd get this wild."

"It's not your fault," Jake told him. "I appreciate you informing us that he'd be here tonight."

Mitch threw his hands in the air as if he were under arrest. "Just so you know, I have *no* idea what was inside that envelope Ben stole. Once we got kicked off the tour and sent home, he sat in the back of the bus without saying a word. And another thing. He was the one who invited us to the vineyard, which was shocking, considering I've never once seen the man drink wine. Places like this are his thing. Grimy dive bars where the beer flows like water and hard drinks are strong and cheap."

"Hold on, back up a minute," Miles said. "Going on the tour of Vincent Vineyard was Ben's idea?"

"Yeah. So was breaking into Don's office. Thing is, Dylan and I didn't know it was a break-in to begin with. Ben told us that he has ties to the Vincent family, and one of them asked him to go in there and get those papers."

"Did he mention which family member?"

"No, not that I can recall."

Jake grabbed a napkin and wiped beads of perspiration from his forehead. Fatigue had begun to set in as the stifling, smoky air constricted his lungs. "Sounds to me like Ben invited you two there to be his fall guys."

"Same thing I was thinking. And we both fell for it. But I shouldn't be surprised. The man is a con artist—" Mitch stopped abruptly when Ben came bursting through the kitchen door.

"Sorry for the interruption, my friends!" he boomed.

"You seem to be in a much better mood than you were before that phone call," Miles said.

"I am. You know why? Because that was my attorney. And he advised me not to say another word to either of you." He pointed across the table at Mitch, his thin lips curled into a snarky smirk. "Hey, man. Did you know that we don't *have* to talk to the police? We can refuse to answer their questions and just refer them to our attorneys!"

Jake looked on in disgust as Ben grabbed a pitcher of beer and guzzled it down. He slammed the empty jug onto the table, then crossed one foot over the other.

"Gonna go grab us another round—"

Bam!

Ben crashed to the floor after attempting a double reverse spin. This time, Jake didn't help him up. Instead, he tossed Miles a nod that indicated *let's get the hell out of here.*

"Mitch," Jake said, extending his hand, "it was good running into you."

"Likewise," he muttered, glancing down at Ben. He was still on the floor, thrashing about on his back like an incapacitated cockroach while struggling to stand.

Jake and Miles stepped over him and made their way toward the exit.

"We need to put Ben under surveillance," Miles suggested. "And bring him into the station to formally be questioned. If he feels the need to bring his lawyer, then so be it."

"I agree. Since he's suddenly caught a case of amnesia, I'll be sure to show them both the video footage of him being chased out of Don's office with that envelope in hand. While I'm at it, I'll bring Jada in for questioning first thing in the morning. I am done playing games with these people."

"I like where your head's at, Chief," Miles said, giving him a high five. "But quick question. What if Jada refuses to come in?"

"She won't. Especially when she finds out I know about her connection to Ben."

Before reaching the car, Jake's cell phone pinged. A text notification from Manuel popped up.

"Uh-oh," he uttered, tapping the message. "What do we have here…"

Chief, I don't know what's going on, but Jada has lost it. She's screaming, crying, running up and down the hallways and saying she's done. I heard her mention your name. Tyler managed to calm her down, and now they're in the conference room behind closed doors.

"We've got action," Jake told Miles before replying to the message.

I just met with Ben Foray and Mitch Wilkerson. Between us, Ben and Jada are somehow connected. I need to find out how. Do you have any idea what was inside that envelope Ben stole from Don's office?

Manuel replied within seconds.

I do. I wanted to share this with you in person, but, it was an amendment to Don's Will, stating that he wanted Greer to take over as president of the vineyard in the event that he dies. I was the only one who knew about that document. Or so I thought...

Jake nudged Miles's shoulder. "Check this out," he said, turning the screen toward him before typing a response.

I really need for you to get to the station and talk to me. On record. I understand your loyalty to the Vincent family, but info you're holding on to could solve this case. You owe it to Don and everyone else to bring justice to his killer.

You're absolutely right. I will be there before the end of the week. You have my word.

The brothers shared a fist bump before climbing inside the car.

"You were right," Miles said. "Manuel has been holding out on us."

"I'm just glad he's finally willing to talk. Prepare for this case to be blown wide open."

Chapter Eleven

Ella slid her palm across the linen tablecloth and intertwined her fingers with Jake's.

"Thank you," she murmured.

"Thank me? For what?"

"For tonight. Inviting me out to this nice dinner. I needed it. We both needed it."

"I agree. And you don't have to thank me, sweetheart. It's my pleasure."

The week had been a long one, and it was only Wednesday. From Jake's run-in with Ben to Jada lawyering up and refusing a police interview, frustrations were mounting. Ella had practically confined herself to the loft after fear of another attack took over. With Charlotte back in River Valley visiting their parents, she'd been spending her days doing investigative work and practicing new relaxation techniques recommended by her therapist.

"This place is nice, isn't it?" Jake asked, glancing around the restaurant. "Fancy French château with servers dressed in tuxedos, serving up delicious signature dishes and custom wine blends."

"It's beautiful. The silk brocade drapes, crystal chandeliers and stone wood-burning fireplace are definitely giving off castle vibes."

"Well, that would be fitting, considering you're a queen and all."

Ella shifted in her seat at the sight of Jake's sexy half smile. "Why are you giving me that look you know makes me swoon?"

"Because… I was just thinking."

"About what?"

"About us. And our future. I know you came to Clemmington to get away from everything that went down in River Valley. But it seems as though you're enjoying your time here. Am I right?"

"You are. Clemmington is a nice change of pace. I've lived in River Valley my entire life. Even though I move around temporarily for work, it's all I've known. But, yeah," she murmured, staring out at the ornamental garden surrounding a marble tiered fountain. "I'm definitely enjoying being here."

"Good." Jake ran his fingertips along the top of her hand. "That's what I like to hear. I'm serious about this relationship, El. You know how much I love you, and from what I've been told, the feeling is mutual."

"It definitely is."

"I think it's clear that we want to make a life together. We've both been out here long enough to know what a good thing looks like, and that once you get it, you don't let it go. Plus, Clemmington General Hospital is always hiring."

"So what exactly are you saying, Mr. Love?"

"What I'm saying is, I want to settle down. I mean *all* the way down. Get married. Start a family. And I can only see myself doing those things with you."

Same here, Ella wanted to respond. But the words refused to escape her lips. Because she had yet to reveal the news that could change Jake's mind about everything.

He picked up his glass and held it in the air. "Come on, grab your wine. We forgot to make a toast. To us. May our relationship continue to grow, prosper and reach new heights. I am so grateful for you, Ella. Being hired as chief of police, then taking on the biggest case of my career... I don't know if I could've done any of it without you. So, thank you. For being here, for supporting me and, most of all, for loving me."

Ella pressed her napkin against her cheeks, catching tears as they trickled from her eyes. "Babe, thank *you*. For all of that. I don't know if my words will stack up to yours. But I'm happy to be here by your side, loving you, supporting you in any way that I can and experiencing this journey with you. I know it isn't easy. And I hope you realize I wouldn't have made it through all that I have without you. Whether you know it or not, you saved me. So, here's to us as we continue to love, support and cover one another."

"Cheers."

As the pair sipped from their glasses, Ella stared at Jake. The love in his shining eyes punctured a hole of guilt through her chest. She felt like a fraud for claiming to adore someone despite not having been completely honest.

"Hey," Jake said. "Are you okay?"

"I'm fine," she lied, the tears she'd cried transforming from joyous to fearful.

"You sure? Because you just did that thing that you've been doing a lot lately."

"What thing?"

Jake released her hand and pointed at her face, drawing an invisible circle. "That thing where you space out, and your thoughts go somewhere deep inside your head. It's as if you've been hypnotized, and you're in some sort of trance."

"Really? *Hmm*," Ella uttered, her furrowed brows feigning confusion. "I didn't realize I'd been doing that." She slid the last of her seared duck breast and sesame ginger zucchini onto her fork and shoved it inside her mouth to avoid any further explanation. A surge of relief hit when Jake swallowed down the final bite of his elk loin, his expression still filled with happiness.

The server approached with dessert menus in hand. "Mademoiselle, monsieur? I hope that you enjoyed your main courses."

"We certainly did," Jake told him. "Everything was amazing."

"Wonderful. I am delighted to hear that. Can I interest either of you in one of our custom desserts?"

Despite being completely stuffed, Ella scanned the menu, wishing she could order everything from the lime and basil tart to the pecan-crusted coconut cheesecake.

"They all sound delicious to me," Jake said. "Which would you recommend?"

"Every offering is delectable, but if I had to choose one, I'd select the classic vanilla crème brûlée topped with citrus segments."

"Now that sounds scrumptious," Ella said. "I'd love to top off my dinner with it."

"Make that two," Jake told the server.

"Yes, monsieur. I will be back shortly. Oh, and my apologies. I forgot to mention that the desserts are complimentary."

"Really?" Jake replied. "That is so nice of the chef. Please tell him we said thank you."

"Ahh, but these were not gifted by the chef. They are being sent compliments of your friends, Tyler and Jada Vincent."

Ella's stomach dropped to the floor. She swiveled in her chair, frantically searching the restaurant for the pair.

"Oh," Jake uttered, also looking around. "Well then, we'll be sure to thank them personally before we leave. Where are they sitting?"

"Upstairs. In our private dining area. You can't see them, but they can see you. I'll be back shortly with your crème brûlée."

"Thank you." Jake waited until he walked away before turning Ella. "Interesting. And somewhat creepy, right? *You can't see them, but they can see you.* So Tyler and Jada have been watching us the whole time we've been here?"

"Apparently so." Ella shivered at the thought of being spied on. Especially by those two. "Now I feel exposed. Violated even."

"Come on now. Don't let them hold that much power over you."

Easy for you to say, Ella thought. Not only did Tyler and Jada have power over her, but they were using the moment to exert it. Knowing they were there was triggering. It transported Ella's mind back to the attack in the corn maze, the chase through the park, the hunt inside the parking garage…

You're doing it again. Deflect. Deep breaths. Think of a beach, a mountainside, glistening white ski slopes.

"I guess we should still find out where this private dining area is located," Jake said, "and personally thank them for the desserts."

"Why?"

"Because I want them to see that I'm not moved by Jada lawyering up and refusing to talk to law enforcement."

An icy chill spun around Ella at the thought of coming face-to-face with the pair.

Play sick, she thought. *Have the server wrap up the desserts to go and get the hell out of here.*

"I need to run to the men's room. Be right back."

Ella barely acknowledged the soft kiss he planted on her cheek before leaving the table. Once Jake was gone, she discreetly eyed the restaurant's second level. A glass staircase led to a stone wall. The dining area had to be on the other side of it. A couple of narrow tinted windows were encased on either end. But there was no door.

Strange…

Something caught her eye near the corner. A crack in the granite appeared. A server slipped through it, revealing a secret door.

"Mademoiselle…"

Ella flinched at the sound of the server's voice. "Yes?"

"Here is your crème brûlée—"

"I'm sorry," she interrupted, holding her hand out before he set them on the table, "but Jake and I just realized that we need to leave. Would you mind wrapping those to go?"

"I'd be happy to. I'll bring the check as well."

Ella reached inside her purse and pulled out her credit card. "Here you go. You can take care of that now. Thank you."

"You're quite welcome. Also…" He reached inside his jacket pocket and pulled out a white envelope. "This note was left for you at the hostess stand, Ms. Bowman."

How does he know my name?

She glanced down at it. There was her answer. Ella's name had been written on the front.

"Do you know who left this?" she asked.

"My apologies, but I do not. I was in the kitchen when it was delivered. I know you and Chief Love are in a hurry, mademoiselle. I will return with your wrapped desserts momentarily."

She nodded, her chest pounding as she tore open the envelope.

Dear Ms. Bowman,
It was mighty bold of you to rear your ugly head here tonight at a Vincent fam-

ily staple. Your days are numbered. Enjoy the dessert. And know that there is nothing sweet about what I've got planned for you. Welcome to the jungle, bitch.

XO,
Me

Ella's vision blurred as she reread the card over and over again.

"The desserts haven't arrived yet?" Jake asked.

She bolted from her chair so abruptly that her head banged against his chin.

"*Ouch!*"

"Jake!" she squealed, clutching the sides of his face. "I am so sorry. I didn't see you come back from the men's room. You...you startled me."

"I was going in for a kiss and instead damn near got knocked out!"

As he wiggled his jaw from side to side, the server came rushing over. "Is everything all right? Monsieur, do you need medical attention?"

"No, no, I'm fine. Maybe an ice pack, but I can take care of that once I get home."

"Very well. Here is your receipt. Once again, thank you for dining with us this evening, and we look forward to seeing you again. Have a wonderful evening."

"Receipt," Jake said. "But I didn't pay the check yet. And we haven't had dessert."

"Tonight is on me," Ella told him, quickly shoving the note deep inside her purse. "And I suddenly started feeling a little headachy. So I asked to have the desserts wrapped up to go."

"Well, don't I feel special. Thank you, my love."

"You're welcome. Now let's get home so I can pop a couple of aspirin, and you can put some ice on your—"

"Wait!" Jake interrupted, turning to the server. "Before you go, would you mind showing us to the private area where Tyler and Jada are dining?"

Dammit! Ella wanted to scream.

"Monsieur, my apologies. But Mr. and Mrs. Vincent left about five minutes ago."

"Oh, okay then," Jake said. "I guess we'll just have to catch them next time."

Ella's feet almost broke into a happy dance as she and Jake walked hand in hand toward the exit. But then, the thought of running into Tyler and Jada in the parking lot crossed her mind.

Stop it. They should be gone by now.

Nevertheless, Ella knew the past was closing in on her. She'd soon have to admit the truth to Jake. At this point, it wasn't just their relationship at risk. It was her life.

Chapter Twelve

Jake bit down on his thumbnail, his feet tapping rapidly against the floor. He checked his watch again. Manuel was almost an hour late. He promised he'd be at the police station first thing in the morning, before checking in at the vineyard.

The chief glared across the interrogation room table at Miles. "Can you believe this guy? He just emailed me yesterday. Gave me his word that he'd be here today. What type of hold do the Vincents have on him that's preventing this meeting from happening?"

"Money. Job security. Loyalty."

"But what about his loyalty to Don?"

"*Humph.*" Miles squinted, staring up at the ceiling as if the answers lay in the white fiberglass tiles. "Not to sound cold, but real talk? Don isn't here anymore. Therefore, Manuel's allegiance is going to be with whoever's signing his paycheck."

"That's just sad."

"It is. But as the saying goes, the truth hurts."

There was a knock at the door.

"*Finally*," Jake said, jumping up from his chair. "Time to get some answers." He swung open the door. Their administrative assistant, Lucy, was standing on the other side.

"Lucy, what's going on?"

"Gina Ruiz is here," she panted, her olive complexion a pale shade of gray.

"Who?"

"Gina Ruiz. Manuel's wife."

"*Okay*," Jake replied, stepping out into the hallway. "Is Manuel with her?"

"No. That's the thing. She said that he's missing."

"Missing? What do you mean *missing*?"

Jake didn't wait for her to respond. He and Miles rushed to the front of the station. When they reached the waiting area, the chief paused at the sight of Gina. She was standing at the front desk, talking to a couple of officers, her body hunched over as tears poured from her swollen eyes.

"But this isn't like him!" she wailed. "Manuel has never spent one night away from me in the twenty-six years that we've been married. I'm telling you, something has happened to him.

And I know those evil Vincents had something to do with it!"

"Mrs. Ruiz," Jake interjected, "I'm Chief Love. I was supposed to meet with your husband here at the station this morning. Did you know about that?"

"No," she whimpered. "I didn't. Ever since Mr. Vincent's murder, Manuel has been keeping so many secrets from me—"

When her voice cracked, Jake held out his arm. "Mrs. Ruiz, please. Follow me to the conference room where we can talk privately. Can I get you anything? Coffee, tea, water?"

"The only thing you can do for me right now is find my husband. *Please*. And bring him home safely."

Once inside the conference room, Jake offered Mrs. Ruiz a seat and set a bottle of water and a box of tissues on the table. A sense of dread burned deep in his gut. It was an instinct he'd possessed for years, and it was never wrong. Someone must've caught wind of Manuel's interview with law enforcement and done something to stop it.

Jake grabbed a blank notebook from the cabinet and sat across from Gina. "Mrs. Ruiz, when was the last time you spoke with your husband?"

"Yesterday evening. At around 6:30 p.m. He said he was heading into an operations meeting with Mrs. Vincent and would be home as soon as they were done."

"Mrs. Vincent, as in Claire Vincent?" Miles asked.

"Yes. *Claire*." The disdain in her tone seeped through stiffened lips.

"Were you and Mrs. Vincent having prob—" Jake began before stopping mid-sentence. He'd find out whether the two women were having issues later. Right now, his number one priority was finding Manuel. "Why didn't you call and report your husband missing at some point during the night since it's so out of character for him not to come home?"

Mrs. Ruiz recoiled in her chair. "Because I… I thought he may have finally given in to Mrs. Vincent's charms and stayed the night with her."

The room fell silent. Only the sound of Jake's creaking chair could be heard as he leaned to the side. "Are you saying that you believe your husband is having some sort of personal relationship with Mrs. Vincent?"

She was slow to respond, first pressing a tissue against her flushed cheeks, then sniffling quietly. "Possibly. I have no proof of it. But those two seem to have grown quite close since Mr. Vincent's murder."

"Well, first things first. We need to find Manuel. We'll start by going to Vincent Vineyard and seeing if any of the family members or employees know of his last whereabouts."

Jake was interrupted when Gina's cell phone pinged. She pulled it from her purse, frantically unlocking the screen while chanting a prayer under her breath.

"Oh, my God!" she screamed.

"What is it, Mrs. Ruiz?"

"It's my son, Daniel. He and his brother Mateo used the location apps on their cell phones to try and locate their father. They're saying he's somewhere near Cypress Creek!"

Muscle spasms ripped through Jake's limbs as he leaped from his chair and hurdled toward the door. "Mrs. Ruiz, please stay here for a moment. Detective Love and I need to alert the other officers."

"No!" she insisted, running after him. "I have to get to that creek and find my husband!"

"It would be much safer if we escort you there. But first I have to pass this information along. Just give me a moment. I'll have Lucy come and sit with you while I assemble my team."

Mrs. Ruiz's head fell as she collapsed against the wall, crying into her hands. After Jake stepped out into the hallway and signaled Lucy inside, he and Miles charged up and down the aisles of the station, alerting his officers of the new development.

"Call the paramedics," Jake said to Officer Underwood. "Tell them to get to Cypress Creek ASAP!"

As the other officers rushed to their squad cars, Jake ran to the crime lab and pounded on the door. Lena threw it open within seconds.

"What's wrong?" she panted, her face covered in goggles and a mask.

"Manuel Ruiz never showed up for his interview. His wife is here, and his sons may have located him somewhere near Cypress Creek. Why don't you ride out there with David and I'll go with Miles. Make sure you bring your master forensics kit. We may have a crime scene on our hands."

JAKE PULLED INTO a clearing near the edge of Cypress Creek's hiking trail. He and Miles hopped out of the car and ran to the trunk, quickly slipping on latex gloves and blue booties before heading toward the woodland.

Officers had already begun stringing yellow crime scene tape along the perimeter. Once Jake and Miles entered the grove, the sun's bright rays disappeared between eighty-foot-tall black oaks' bristled leaves.

The brothers stepped carefully over the trees' oddly shaped roots growing above ground, their feet sinking into the forest floor's damp soil.

Echoes of croaking frogs, buzzing insects and chirping birds ricocheted through the damp breeze.

"It feels like I'm walking through a jungle," Miles said.

"Yeah, which is exactly why I'm glad Mrs. Ruiz decided to stay back at the station. She didn't need to be out here. Especially if we end up finding Manuel's body."

The pair approached a group of officers searching the edge of the creek.

"Anything turn up so far?" Jake asked David.

"Nothing yet. We're keeping an eye out for anything viable. A shoe, a pair of glasses, a cell phone…anything that may lead us to Mr. Ruiz."

Jake took a quick look around the vicinity. "Where is Lena? She was supposed to ride here with you."

"She did. But she's gonna hang back in the car for a bit. Just between us, I think she might still be struggling after everything she went through with the Heart-Shaped Murders investigation. Since she spends most of her time in the forensics lab these days, being out here might be triggering. So I told her we'd call if we need her."

"Good idea. But hopefully we won't—"

A gut-wrenching scream whirred through the air.

"Help! *Help!*" someone yelling in the distance.

Jake and his officers took off running in the direction of the shouting.

"Who's there?" Jake called out. "And where are you?"

"It's Daniel and Mateo Ruiz! We're over by the west end of the creek!"

Miles grabbed Jake's arm and pointed up ahead. "This way!"

The excruciating cries grew closer. And louder.

This can't be good, Jake thought, a sick feeling pooling inside his chest.

He and the team continued running at full speed, pushing past low-hanging branches while leaping over hollows hidden within the dirt.

"Should I call Lena and tell her to get out here?" David heaved.

"Yes!" Jake yelled right before his phone buzzed. The call was coming from the police station.

"Chief Love speaking."

"Chief! It's Lucy."

He could barely hear her for all the screaming in the background.

"You're gonna have to speak up, Lucy!"

"Can you hear me now?" she shrieked.

"Yes! What's going on?"

"Mrs. Ruiz's sons just called her. They think they've found their father's body floating in the creek! Where are you?"

"We're looking for them now. Tell Mrs. Ruiz that we're handling it and I'll contact her once we know more."

"Okay, got it."

Jake peered up ahead. Two young men who looked to be in their late teens clung to one another near the water's edge.

"I think I see Mr. Ruiz's sons!" Miles said.

The chief sped up, fighting off the cramps tightening his leg.

When the young men noticed law enforcement heading their way, they charged toward them, jumping wildly in the air while pointing toward the water.

"He's over here!" they yelled.

Daniel and Mateo led them to a body floating near the bank of the creek.

"Oh, my God," Miles choked, covering his mouth.

A swarm of fathead minnows darted around Manuel's thick black hair as it swayed in the current. His white shirt was pulled up to his neck, exposing his bloated pale back. Jagged bite marks covered his skin, inflicted by scavenging creatures feeding on his corpse. An infestation of blowflies hovered over his body, crawling along the flesh in search of a perfect spot to lay eggs.

One of Mr. Ruiz's sons ran toward the water,

almost reaching the body before his brother pulled him back.

"Guys!" Jake said, wrapping his arms around both men and guiding them away from the creek. "Please, I know this is tough. But you're gonna have to let us do our jobs and figure out what happened here. By the way, I'm Chief Love. I'll be handling the investigation. And I am so sorry that this has happened to your father."

"Who would've done this to him?" one of the brothers cried. "Why would some maniac kill our dad?"

"That's exactly what we're going to find out. In the meantime, I'd like for you both to head to the police station with Officer Underwood. He's going to ask you some questions. Your mom is there too, and I'm sure she needs you right now. I'll check in with you shortly. Okay?"

They nodded, leaning on one another as Officer Underwood escorted them away from the crime scene.

Miles placed a hand of support on Jake's shoulder. "I just called the medical examiner's office. He's on the way."

"Good, thanks." Jake instructed a couple of officers to continue cordoning off the area, reminding everyone not to disturb the body. Just as Detective Campbell began taking photos of the scene, Lena and David ran up.

She stared out into the creek, shaking her head while eyeing the victim. "What are you thinking? That someone found out Mr. Ruiz was coming to speak with law enforcement and got to him before he got to you?"

"That's exactly what I'm thinking," Jake replied.

"Well, I'd better get in here and start processing the scene. I'll keep you posted and let you know if I find anything worthwhile. Miles, did I just hear you say that the medical examiner is on his way?"

"Yes, he is."

"All right." Lena pulled several brown paper bags and a metal scalpel from her forensics kit. "I'll be over by the water, gathering samples of the soil near Mr. Ruiz's body. Once the medical examiner removes him from the water, I'll collect his clothing along with any trace and biological evidence I can find. Fingernail clippings, blood evidence, wounds, bite marks…"

Jake pulled his father's white monogrammed handkerchief from his pocket, which he'd passed down for good luck, and wiped his face. "Sounds good. I'll be circling the area, searching for evidence and keeping an eye on things. Give me a holler if you need me."

Lena gave him a thumbs-up before setting off toward the creek. "Fingers crossed there's something viable here. We need it. Especially after the reexamination of evidence from Don's crime scene didn't render any new results."

"Yes, we do," Jake grumbled, still disappointed by that news.

He found a quiet area away from all the chaos and called Ella. She picked up on the first ring.

"Hey, babe. How did it go with Manuel this morning?"

He opened his mouth to speak. But the words just wouldn't come out.

"Hello? Jake, are you still here? *Dammit*, I think I lost you."

"No, I'm still here."

"Uh-oh. You don't sound too good. What's wrong? Please don't tell me that Manuel didn't show up."

"No, he didn't show up. Because he's—"

"Wait," Ella interrupted, "don't tell me. Let me guess. Manuel lawyered up too, didn't he? See, I cannot believe how these people are trying to avoid being—"

"*Ella*. Listen to me. Manuel didn't show up because he's…he's dead."

The other end of the phone went silent. Jake waited for her to say something. But after several moments, there was still no response.

"El? You there?"

"I… I'm here," she stammered. "This is just…

unreal. Manuel is dead? What is happening? I feel like I'm reliving a nightmare all over again. First it was the Numeric Serial Killer, and now this!"

Jake pressed his fist against his forehead, wondering if he'd made the wrong move.

You shouldn't have called her with this news. You should have waited until you got home. Told her in person.

But he knew it was only a matter of time before the media caught wind of Manuel's death. He'd rather Ella find out about it from him than some random reporter.

"Listen," he said. "I don't want you to get upset. I just want you to be aware of what's going on. We still don't know exactly what happened to him. But his body was found floating in Cypress Creek, by his sons, unfortunately. I've got all of law enforcement out here with me and we're waiting on the medical examiner to arrive. Once he does, I'll know more."

"Does Charlotte know yet?"

"I doubt it. Miles is busy examining the crime scene with Lena, and I'm pretty sure the news hasn't hit the media yet."

"So what's next, Jake? How in the hell are you going to catch whoever's doing this? I mean, it's obviously someone connected to Vincent Vineyard. But who?"

"That's what we're all here working to find out. I said it before and I'll say it again. I'm done playing mister nice guy. I am not doing any more polite rounds of questioning or interviews on anybody else's turf. I'll be conducting interrogations down at the station, with lie detector tests to boot. And you'd better believe I'll be obtaining a search warrant, giving me full access to the vineyard. And if Manuel was in fact murdered, let's just hope the killer left some sort of DNA evidence behind—"

"*Chief*!" Lena called out. "I need you over here. I've got something!"

"I'll be right there!"

Ella moaned into the phone. "I heard all that. Be careful, babe. And please, keep me posted on any new updates that you get. In the meantime, I'll reach out to Charlotte and let her know what's going on."

"Thanks. Love you."

"Love you too."

A surge of energy shot through Jake as he rushed over toward the edge of the creek. He crouched down next to Lena, observing the small coin envelope she was holding.

"What have you got there?" he asked.

"Shell casings. Four of them. Looks like they're twenty-two caliber long rifles."

Jake peered inside the envelope and studied

the contents. "So Manuel may have been shot to death?"

"Possibly. Either that, or he drowned. While we wait on the medical examiner to provide that information, I'll test these casings for DNA."

"How can you do that?" an officer asked who'd been hovering behind them.

"Easy," Lena replied. "First, I'll soak them in a tube of mixed chemicals that will break open cells that could identify a suspect. I'll also enter the serial numbers into the National Integrated Ballistics Information Network and compare the cartridges to those that are already in the system. You never know. They may end up connecting to another crime that's been committed."

"That would be great," Jake said. "I'm so glad we're using the NIBIN now. Since those casings look to be made of brass, you may be able to lift fingerprints off of them too, right?"

"That is correct. I've taught you well." Lena turned toward the creek, squinting as she stared out at Manuel's body. "It'll be interesting to hear the results of the autopsy. Speaking of which, I wonder when the medical examiner is going to get here. I really want to start lifting evidence from the body."

No sooner than the words were out of her mouth, Dr. Lynn and two of his transporters were allowed past the crime scene tape.

"Chief Love, Ms. Love, it's good to see you both, despite the grim circumstances, of course."

"Dr. Lynn," Jake said, standing and shaking his hand. "It's good to see you as well."

The medical examiner pointed toward the water. "Has the victim been identified yet?"

"He has. His name is Manuel Ruiz. The body hasn't been disturbed. We're thinking that he was attacked in some way and left for dead. Lena just found several shell casings near the edge of the water, not too far from the body."

"Good to know. Once we remove him from the creek, we'll be able to get a better look and possibly figure out how he lost his life. I'll search for ligature marks, stab wounds, bullet wounds… You know the drill. Of course, I'll have more definitive answers once the body is transferred to my office and a full autopsy is performed."

"Absolutely. I'll get out of your way and let you get to it. Lena will be working with you as she collects biological evidence from the body. If either of you need me, I'll be in the vicinity. Please, keep me updated on any pertinent findings."

"Will do." Lena gave his shoulder a reassuring nudge. He responded with a nod of thanks, then watched as Dr. Lynn photographed Manuel's body. The medical examiner's assistants pulled several white linen sheets from their equipment case, along with a black vinyl body bag, rolls of tape and brown paper bags.

Once Dr. Lynn was done taking pictures, he and his team pulled Manuel's body from the water and laid him on his back. Jake's stomach twisted into knots at the sight of his swollen, disfigured face, which had been mangled by ravenous aquatic creatures. Right below a particularly deep bite mark on the left side of his chest were two small red holes.

Lena turned to Jake and pointed toward the wounds just as Miles walked up.

"What's the latest?" the detective asked.

"Lena found several shell casings near Manuel's body. And there looks to be gunshot wounds in his chest."

"*Humph*. The plot thickens…"

"And all roads are leading back to those Vincent brothers. We just need to figure out which one of them is willing to kill for the vineyard's top spot."

Chapter Thirteen

Charlotte pulled in front of Clemmington General Hospital and put the car in Park.

"Are you sure you don't want me to come inside with you?" she asked Ella.

"I'm positive. I'll be fine. Bringing me here was more than enough."

"Okay, well, I'll be waiting for you when you're done." Before Ella stepped out of the car, Charlotte grabbed her arm. "Wait, do you really think this is a good idea? I mean, you've been through so much already. Taking on a full-time job right now may be too overwhelming, don't you think?"

Ella fell against the back of the seat. "For the tenth time, Charlotte, no. I don't think taking on a full-time job would be too much for me. I need this. I cannot continue to just sit around Jake's loft, digging through the same case files over and over again in search of new leads. Nursing is my passion. It takes me away from all the madness that's happening around me. Even my therapi—" She paused, remembering that she hadn't told Charlotte she'd been in counseling. "I mean, working with patients is therapeutic. It'll be good for me."

"Well, if going back to work is something you need in your life so badly, why didn't you tell Jake about this meeting with the hospital administrator?"

"I love how you're acting like we haven't been through this already. I'm not one of your suspects, Charlotte. Constantly asking me the same questions isn't going to change my answers. Now, for the last time, I'm planning on surprising Jake with the news once I get the job. He and I talked about me moving to Clemmington permanently and taking on a full-time job. This is my way of showing him that I'm serious about it."

"Okay, fine," Charlotte snipped. "You know, you've been acting really weird lately. Like there's something going on that you're not telling me. Are you sure you're not hiding anything?"

Ella's head swiveled as she stared straight ahead at the hospital's redbrick exterior. Lying to her sister had never come easy. The older they got, the harder it became. "No, Char. I am not hiding anything from you. Now can I please go inside before I'm late?"

"Yes. Go on. I'll try and find a space near the entrance so you won't miss me when you come out. Good luck, Nurse Bowman."

"Thanks, sis."

Ella bolted from the car and practically ran through the hospital's automatic glass doors. The relief of being out from underneath Charlotte's scrutiny was eclipsed by a bout of guilt.

You have got to confess your secret to somebody. Why not let it be your own sister?

But as the Vincent Vineyard murder mystery deepened, Ella grew wearier of discussing her past with anyone. Including Charlotte. After Manuel's murder, the entire town of Clemmington was up in arms, feeling as though they may have another serial killer on their hands. Ella, however, refused to sit around wondering whether or not she'd be next. She had to get out and live. Being cooped up alone while waiting for the next threat to drop had become unbearable.

Just focus on this moment and getting the job, Ella thought as she approached the reception desk.

"Good morning, ma'am," a plump older woman with a fire-engine red pixie cut said without looking up from her computer screen. "How may I help you?"

"Good morning. My name is Ella Bowman.

I'm here to meet with the hospital administrator, Bernadette Stevens."

The woman's acrylic French tips click-clacked across her keyboard as she searched for the appointment in her system. "All right, Ms. Bowman. Here's a visitor's pass. The elevators are straight back behind the reception desk and to your right. Mrs. Stevens's office is located on the third floor. Once you arrive, please let her assistant know that you're here for your 10:00 a.m. meeting, and she'll take it from there."

"Will do. Thank you."

Ella glanced around the facility as she made her way to the elevator banks. It was modest, with its stark white walls and speckled beige tile. Scenic watercolor paintings served as the decor, while artificial birch trees and pale blue furniture filled the lobby. The staff seemed friendly enough, smiling and greeting everyone from coworkers to visitors as they passed one another. The vibe was simple, but cozy.

I could get used to this...

When the elevator arrived, Ella stepped on and headed to the third floor. As soon as the doors opened, a young blonde woman wearing turquoise cat-eye glasses and a huge smile bellowed, "Hello, Ella Bowman?" before hopping up from her chair.

"Yes!" Ella boomed more enthusiastically

than she'd intended. She blamed it on the receptionist's big cheerleader energy.

"It's so nice to meet you! But…" She paused, propping her fist underneath her chin while putting on a dramatic pout. "I do have a bit of bad news."

"Oh, no. Don't tell me. The neonatal nurse position has already been filled?"

"No, no, nothing like that. Mrs. Stevens just had a family emergency and left a few minutes ago." The woman plopped back down into her chair, grabbing the desk before she rolled back into the wall. She snatched a sticky note off her computer monitor and slowly read from it. "Mrs. Stevens sends her apologies, asked that I thank you for filling out the job application online, and said she'll email you to reschedule today's meeting."

A pang of disappointment stirred inside Ella's head. The neonatal unit was looking to fill the position immediately. She'd hoped to land the job today and start as soon as possible.

"Okay then," Ella muttered, taking a step back toward the elevator. "Thank you, and I, um… I guess I'll just keep an eye out for Mrs. Stevens's message—"

"Wait!" the woman shouted before jumping back up. "I have an idea. Since you're already here, why don't you go up and take a look at the

NICU? You know, so that today won't feel like a wasted visit."

Ella clasped her hands together, her spirits lifting at the suggestion. "I would love to. Thank you. Where is the unit located?"

"Just one floor up. On four. I would take you myself, but we're so short-staffed, and I'm pretty much working this floor alone. But you'll be fine. I'll call and let the receptionist know you're on the way."

"I really appreciate this. Thanks again."

After stepping back onto the elevator, Ella arrived on the fourth floor within seconds. The receptionist was on a call but waved her through the heavy metal door.

She entered the hallway, her ears perking at the familiar sounds of patient monitors ringing and alarms pinging throughout the unit. The bright green walls and shiny hardwood floors appeared more vibrant than the hospital's sterile lobby—a nice touch for parents in distress.

Ella peeked inside the patient rooms, clutching her chest as she eyed the incubators housing newborn babies. Being there felt cathartic, comforting even. It was a reminder of where she belonged.

She tiptoed along the corridor, silencing the loud heels on her shoe boots, while everyone on the floor spoke in hushed voices. Two nurses standing outside a room whispered to one another, their grinning expressions filled with joy.

"Yes!" one of them exclaimed. "Baby Melinda started breathing on her own today and was transferred upstairs to the nursery."

Aww, the nursery! Ella almost blurted out. She smiled at the women and continued down the hallway, staring at a stairwell door once she reached the end of the corridor.

Her feet shuffled back and forth. She was itching to go up to the nursery and lay eyes on the babies.

No one would mind, she thought, already considering herself an employee.

Before giving it another thought, Ella crept into the stairwell and took two steps at a time up to the fifth floor.

She cracked open the door, sticking her head inside and taking a look around the bustling unit before entering. Its green walls and shiny floors resembled that of the NICU. Doctors and nurses scampered up and down the hall, zooming past visitors carrying bouquets of flowers and new moms getting in a little exercise.

Ella approached the nursery, swooning at all the chubby-faced babies swathed in blankets.

"Aww," she breathed, her forehead pressed against the glass.

"They're adorable, aren't they?" someone asked.

She spun around, startled by the question. But when she saw what appeared to be a loving grandmother, her defenses settled.

"They sure are," Ella gushed. "I'm a nurse, hoping to get a job here inside the NICU. This is the part I miss most. The newborns."

The woman came closer, pointing at a little girl swaddled in a fluffy pink blanket. "There's my grandbaby. Bonnie Nicole. She is such a sweet girl. Quiet, already breastfeeding, sleeping well… Nothing like her mother, who was colicky, didn't latch for quite some time and refused to sleep through the night. *Whew!* I certainly don't miss those days."

"Well, at least you'll have a different experience this go round. Congratulations to you."

"Thank you so much. I'd better get back to my daughter's room and check on her. Good luck with that nursing job."

As the woman walked away, Ella suddenly remembered that Charlotte was outside waiting for her.

She set off down the hallway in search of the elevator banks. The west wing corridor's stairwell came into view first. Ella figured she'd stop back down on the third floor and thank Mrs. Stevens's receptionist before leaving.

After giving the unit one last look, Ella slipped inside the stairwell, feeling confident in her decision to return to work. She bounced down the concrete stairs, the sound of her heels echoing loudly off the industrial gray walls. For a brief moment, the memory of being chased inside the casino's parking garage flashed through her mind.

Nope! she told herself, immediately deflecting.

Thoughts of the nursery's sweet babies overrode the chase. Ella focused on the newborns until she reached the third floor. She grabbed the handle and pulled the door. It didn't open. She tried again, a little harder this time. It didn't budge.

What the hell?

Ella gave it a few more yanks before giving up and running to the fourth floor. She tried that door. It too was locked. She felt herself growing hot as her breathing quickened.

Stay calm...

She pulled out her cell phone and called Charlotte. Three beeps chirped in her ear.

Call failed.

Ella looked around. The ceilings, floors and walls were all made of cement. There were no windows. It was as if she were inside a bomb shelter.

Of course. No reception.

She stared at the door. It was painted gray,

not white like the one she'd seen on the way up to the fifth floor. The vinyl decal with the floor number was black, not silver like the others.

That's when it dawned on her. Ella had used the east wing stairwell to go up from the third to the fourth and fifth floors, then got turned around in the maternity ward and took the wrong stairwell back down.

"That's okay," she told herself, ignoring the rumble of fear bubbling inside her stomach. "This is an easy fix."

She knocked on the door, praying that someone on the other side could hear her.

"Hello?" Ella called out.

No response.

"Hello!" she tried again, louder this time. Her knocking turned into banging as her anxiety increased.

Once again, nothing.

"Forget this," Ella uttered, charging down the stairs while convincing herself that the first-floor door would be unlocked. It wasn't.

"Hey!" she screamed. Prickling pain shot up her arm as she pounded on the door. "I'm locked in the stairwell! Can anybody hear me?"

Still, no response.

Ella squeezed the burgundy metal railing and glanced down. There were a few more sets of stairs below. After running the three flights, hitting the landing and practically falling into the door, she grabbed the handle.

"*Please* let this one be unlocked," she whispered, twisting the lever and pulling back. This time, it opened.

Her chest heaved with relief. "Thank you!"

Ella stepped inside the room, unable to see through the darkness. The door slammed behind her. She winced, blinking rapidly to adjust her vision.

Several bleak corridors appeared up ahead. The concrete floor was covered in dust, and yellow caution tape hung from the doors. Do Not Enter and Construction Zone signs were scattered everywhere. A flickering exit sign hung above a door in the far distance. Ella made a run for it. She reached the halfway point.

Boom!

A door slammed behind her. She stopped abruptly. And waited.

Silence.

Ella spun around. A sharp gasp caught in her throat. She held the cough threatening to escape her lips, searching for some sign of movement. There was none.

Turn around and get the hell out of here!

She set off toward the exit, her muscles throbbing as her boots pounded the concrete.

"Excuse me, ma'am?" a strange voice rasped behind her.

Do not stop. You're almost there!

"Ma'am! Is everything all right? I heard banging inside the stairwell, and when I checked the second floor, you were already heading down to the basement."

Ella slowed down a bit and glanced over her shoulder. A figure was jogging toward her dressed in scrubs, a white lab coat, surgical hat, mask and gloves.

"*Oh, thank God*," she cried out, falling against the wall while panting uncontrollably. "I got locked inside the stairwell and freaked out. So I ran down here. All I'm trying to do is leave the hospital."

"You poor thing," the doctor murmured, moving in closer. "I'm so sorry that happened to you. Since this area has been blocked off, all the doors are locked. Come with me. I'll show you where you can exit. It certainly isn't down here. This area is under construction and restricted to the public."

"Thank you so much," Ella breathed, trying to get a better look at the person. The voice sounded strained, as if they had just undergone throat surgery. The scrubs and lab coat were ill-fitting, appearing way too big. But the downturned brown eyes behind the goggles—they appeared somewhat familiar.

"You're welcome. Follow me."

Ella hesitated. The tingling in her gut set off an alarm inside her head. Something wasn't right.

The doctor spun around. "You coming? Or do you wanna stay down here and let the bogeyman get you? Ha!"

Ella jumped at the doctor's sinister laughter. *That wasn't funny*, she almost spewed.

"Sorry," the doctor snorted. "That's a running joke between my kids and me. I guess it just popped into my head since Halloween is right around the corner."

"You know what?" Ella said, slowly backing away. "I think I'm gonna just try this door down here instead of going back upstairs. The sign above it says it's an exit, so I'll take my chances and see where it leads me."

The doctor's head swiveled. Ella didn't wait for a response. She turned and headed toward the door, struggling to walk at a normal pace so as not to appear frightened.

"Suit yourself!" the doctor called out.

Behind her, Ella heard footsteps thumping. But they weren't going in the opposite direction. They were coming after her.

"*Ellaaa*," the doctor sang out. "You're not gonna get away from me this time!"

Her calm stride transformed into a frantic sprint. Tears sprang from Ella's eyes as reality hit. Her attacker was following her every move, even hunting her down inside the hospital.

Will I make it out alive this time?

The exit was a just few feet away. Ella reached out, her fingertips inches away from the handle.

"Gotcha!" the assailant screamed before jumping onto her back.

Ella's body slammed against the concrete floor. She cried out in pain. "Help! *Please*, somebody help me!"

The attacker pressed his mouth against Ella's ear. She cringed as his sharp wet teeth grazed her lobe. "Shut up before I slice your throat open!" The threat was backed up by a cold jagged piece of metal pressed against her neck.

"Why are you doing this to me?" Ella hissed. "What do you *want*?"

"I want you to get the hell out of Clemmington before I tell everyone your nasty little secret. You know what you did." He flipped her over onto her back and took hold of her neck. "Unless you wanna end up like Manuel…"

"No!" Ella screamed, flinching underneath the weight of his body as excruciating pain shot up her spine. She let out one last cry for help before the grip on her throat intensified. Ella choked, her head tightening as the blood vessels in her face pulsated.

The attacker squeezed her lower half between his thighs while his elbows dug into her chest. Barely able to move, she attempted to swing her arms and fight back. But her fists couldn't connect. She was punching the air, wasting her last bits of energy. Her breathing thinned. Ella felt herself fading.

The exit door flew open. Bright sunlight poured into the dimly lit basement. A burly construction worker wearing a red plaid shirt, neon mesh work vest and white hard hat appeared in the doorway.

"Hey!" he yelled. "What are you two doing down here? This area is restricted. Didn't you see all the signs?"

Ella's attacker jumped up and backed away. "Yes, we did. But this woman was in distress. I was attempting CPR. However, she seems fine now."

No! Ella tried to scream. But the hold on her neck had numbed her vocal cords.

"I've got to get back to my patients!" the assailant said before taking off running.

"Yo, Doc!" the construction worker called out. "Didn't I just tell you that you're not supposed to be down here? Exit this way."

But it was too late. He had already ducked back inside the stairwell.

Ella rolled over onto her side, gasping for air while clutching her neck.

"Ma'am, are you all right?"

"No," she whispered. "But I will be."

He bent down and helped her to her feet. She immediately fell against the wall.

"Whoa!" he grabbed her arms, helping to steady her. "Do you need me to escort you up to the emergency room or something?"

"No, I'm fine. Could you just show me the way to the parking lot?"

"Sure," he said. "It's right out here."

He held Ella up as they walked out onto the loading dock, where a group of workers were busy loading wooden planks onto the backs of pickup trucks. She wanted to throw her arms around the man and thank him for saving her life. But she didn't have the energy.

"Are you sure you're okay?" he probed once again. "Do you need me to walk you to your car?"

"I appreciate the offer, but no. I'm fine."

He pointed toward a half-open rolling steel door. "Head straight through there and to the right. The parking lot will be straight ahead."

"Thank you again."

Ella fought through the pain of her attack,

struggling to straighten up and appear normal as she searched for Charlotte's car. A fresh batch of tears threatened to fall at the thought of escaping yet another brutal confrontation. But she held them back. She couldn't let her sister see her upset.

Just get to the car, Ella told herself, ducking down in between the vehicles for fear that her attacker may be watching. The moment she reached Charlotte's sedan, Ella tore open the door and fell into the passenger seat.

"Hey!" Charlotte boomed. "How'd it go? It must've been great considering you were gone for so long. Tell me all about it. Wait! Before you start, just let me apologize for questioning whether or not you're ready to go back to work. Only you can make that decision. Not me, or anyone else for that matter. So, I'm sorry. Now go on. I'm listening."

Ella sat straight up, turned to her sister and burst into tears.

"Oh, honey, what's wrong?" Charlotte embraced her tightly. "You didn't get the job?"

"No, that's not it. Remember earlier, when you said it seems like I've been keeping something from you?"

"I do. Why?"

"Because you were right," Ella muttered. "We've got a lot to talk about."

Chapter Fourteen

"Is your name Jada Vincent?" a polygraph examiner asked.

"Yes."

"Are you the president of the United States?"

"No."

"Have you ever stolen anything?"

"I—um...no. *Wait*. Yes."

Jake stood inside the observation room, looking on as Jada underwent a lie detector test in the interrogation room. The examiner had already told her to stop fidgeting three times. But she continued to wiggle her index and ring fingers, which were covered in black electrodes that measured the skin's sweat and ability to conduct energy.

"She's nervous," Miles said. "Notice how she can't keep still? Her legs are bouncing around all over the place. I guess she doesn't realize all that excess movement will affect her results."

"I don't think Jada is taking any of this seriously. She has no idea we're considering her a person of interest. I'm surprised her attorney even agreed to a polygraph."

"He seems pretty convinced that she's innocent, so that could be it."

Jake peered at the examiner's computer screen. He studied the lines measuring her respiratory rate, electrodermal activity and heart rate. So far, only small lines appeared, indicating her answers were truthful.

"Did you have anything to do with Manuel Ruiz's death?" the examiner asked.

"No."

"Were you born on November tenth?"

"Yes."

"Do you know a man named Ben Foray?"

Jada remained silent. The examiner looked up at her, awaiting a response. The lines on the computer screen enlarged significantly, indicating the question had caused her blood pressure, breathing and perspiration rates to increase.

"Do you know a man named Ben Foray?" the examiner repeated.

"Nuh—uhh…*no*."

"*Wow*," Miles breathed, running his hands down the sides of his face. "I cannot believe she lied about that. What is she hiding?"

"I don't know, but best believe we're gonna find out."

Jada shifted in her chair, the sequins on her yellow bell-bottoms jumpsuit blinging off the walls.

"Did you have anything to do with Don Vincent's murder?" the examiner asked.

"No."

"Are you currently in the state of California?"

"Yes."

"Do you know who killed Don Vincent?"

"No."

Once again, Jake monitored the computer screen. The lines were small, indicating Jada was telling the truth.

"Mrs. Vincent, the polygraph test is complete," the examiner said. "Please remain still while I take the instrument out of operation."

She slumped back in her chair, kicking her clear platform wedges out in front of her.

"Thank *God*," she moaned. "Hurry up and get this stuff off of me! How did I do? Did I pass? Wait, what am I saying? I already know the answer to that. Of course I passed!"

The examiner stood over Jada, removing the black rubber tubes from her chest and abdomen. "I need to speak with law enforcement first. Once I do that, I'll come back in and share the results with you."

"What the hell? Well, can I at least speak to my attorney?" Jada jolted from her chair and swung open the door. "Nick? *Nick!* Get in here. I'm done!"

Jake rushed inside the interrogation room. "Mrs. Vincent, I will send your attorney in momentarily. Joseph," he said to the examiner, "I'll show you to the conference room. We can talk there."

Once everyone was situated in their designated locations, Jake and Miles sat across from Joseph.

"So," Miles said, "how did she do?"

The examiner opened his laptop and pulled up the test results. "Well, there was no deception indicated on any of the questions."

"*Really?*" Jake blurted. "But I saw those lines on the screen increase significantly when you asked Mrs. Vincent whether she—"

"Knew Ben Foray," Joseph finished for him. "I was getting to that. It was the only response that rendered an inconclusive result."

"Inconclusive? Not deceptive?"

"That is correct."

"Interesting…" Jake turned to Miles, his wrinkled expression perplexed. "Why don't we bring Mrs. Vincent in? See what she has to say about this?"

"Let's do it."

The minute Jake hit the hallway, he heard Jada

screaming at the top of her lungs from behind the interrogation room's closed door.

"Listen to me, Nick! My heart was thumping out of my chest the whole damn time! Why would you let me agree to a lie detector test in the first place?"

Jake stood outside the door, listening for her attorney's response.

"Because you're innocent, Mrs. Vincent. I'm telling you, this was a power move on your part. There is not one iota of a doubt in my mind that you passed the test."

"Oh, please. Stop trying to butter me up. I'm not paying you five hundred dollars an hour to kiss my ass. I'm paying you to save it!"

Jake had heard enough. He threw open the door and stuck his head inside. "Mrs. Vincent, Mr. Blackman, the polygraph examiner is ready to reveal the test results. Please, follow me."

Jada, who'd been standing over her attorney with her arms crossed, leaned down and stuck her finger in his face. "You'd better hope these results are in my favor. Because if they're not, and this town finds out and starts spreading rumors that I'm some deranged serial killer, I swear I will beat your—"

"Mrs. Vincent," her attorney interrupted, "why don't we go with Chief Love and wrap things up so you can get back to the vineyard? Didn't you say you have a meeting with…with, um…"

As he headed toward the door, Jada shot visual daggers at his back. "A meeting? What meeting? I never said I had a—"

"We're right behind you, Chief Love," her lawyer interjected, side-eyeing Jada after she failed to catch the bone he'd thrown.

Once Jake led them inside the conference room, Jada tossed her Chanel bag onto the table and threw her arms in the air. "All right, mister polygraph man. Enough with all the suspense. Let's hear it. How did I do?"

"Well, as I told the officers, the majority of your responses rendered a result of no deception indicated."

"Yay! *Wait...*" she sidled up to her attorney and whispered, "What does that mean?"

"That you passed the test."

"*Yes!*" Jada squealed, her sequin pants swishing loudly as she swayed her hips from side to side.

"There was one question, however," the examiner continued, "where the results rendered inconclusive."

The flurry of yellow sparkles stopped mid-swirl. Once again, Jada turned to her lawyer. "Translation, please?"

"An inconclusive result occurs when neither a truthful nor deceptive result is rendered."

"In English, Nick! Is this man saying I didn't score a hundred percent on the test?" Jada charged the table, hovering over the polygraph examiner's laptop. "Which question did I mess up on?"

"The one where I asked whether you know a man named Ben Foray."

Jake paused, observing Jada's reaction.

She gagged, gripping her stomach while covering her mouth. "Nick, let's go," she choked before snatching up her purse and charging the door. "Now!"

"Hold on, Mrs. Vincent," the examiner said. "You can always retake the test and see if your response registers as no deception indicated next time—"

"I will not be retaking a thing," she shot back. "*Nick*. I'm ready to get out of here!"

Her attorney rushed out the door, chasing after Jada as she ranted down the corridor.

"Let's follow them," Jake told Miles. "I don't wanna miss a word of this."

"Right behind you."

Jada's arms swung wildly, her tirade intensifying. "How the hell did Faith pass her lie detector test with flying colors and I didn't, Nick!" Jada fumed. "And that damn Tyler… He is *always* getting me involved in some mess."

"We'll discuss this later, Mrs. Vincent. Preferably outside of the police station."

"I don't give a damn where I'm at. I am pissed! This is my reputation on the line here. All the shady ass schemes Tyler's involved in are gonna land us both in jail—"

"That is enough, Mrs. Vincent! As your legal counsel, I am advising you to keep quiet before you land *yourself* in jail."

As Nick ushered Jada out the door, Jake and Miles stopped at the reception desk.

"What did we just witness?" Miles asked.

"Quite an incriminating outburst," Jake replied. "All this intel, but not enough evidence to draw up charges on anyone. That's the most frustrating part of this investigation. Everybody's whereabouts checked out during the time that Manuel went missing. Claire and Alan were each other's alibi, Tyler and Jada claimed they had eyes on one another throughout the day and night. So did Greer and Faith. All the other vineyard employees' stories checked out too."

"Yeah, well, somebody is lying."

"I agree. But who though?"

Miles leaned over the desk and pulled a piece of licorice from Lucy's candy jar. "That's the million-dollar question. What's our next move, Chief?"

"I need to put in another call to Judge Pierce. Find out when he plans on issuing that search warrant. We have got to get inside Vincent Vineyard. Once we do that, we may very well find our answer."

Chapter Fifteen

The Love family was gathered on Kennedy and Betty's backyard deck in celebration of her birthday. The atmosphere was festive as a silver balloon garland hung from the cedar wood fence, multicolored string lights twinkled within the redbud tree's branches, and a huge bouquet of red roses sat in the center of the table.

Betty's favorite restaurant, The Spicy Cajun Kitchen, had catered the event with several of their specialties—jambalaya, a crawfish boil, deep fried okra, French bread rolls and king cake for dessert.

The setting was perfect. The mood, however, was somber. Despite having promised Betty that there would be no talk of the Vincent Vineyard case, whispers of the investigation buzzed throughout the yard.

"Did Miles tell you that Manuel's autopsy results came in this afternoon?" Ella asked Charlotte.

"No, we haven't really had a chance to talk. I

was at the pediatrician's office all day with Ari for her shots. What did the medical examiner conclude?"

"That Manuel was shot twice in the chest. Once in the rib cage and once in the lung parenchyma. But it wasn't the bullets that killed him since neither hit a major organ or blood vessels."

"So how did he die?"

"He drowned. There was bloody froth found in his airway and a significant amount of water in his stomach."

"*Ooh, that poor man.*" Charlotte's gaze roamed toward the other side of the deck where Jake, Miles, Lena and David were hovered in a corner. "How is Jake doing? He's gotta be extremely stressed out. Trust me, I know what all this feels like firsthand."

"Stressed isn't even the word for it at this point. This case has become a twenty-four-hours-a-day obsession for him. Sleepless nights, early mornings fueled with black coffee and Excedrin Migraine and incessant brainstorming on his next move. I keep a supply of nitroglycerin on hand just in case the man has a heart attack."

"Wait, stick a pin in that for a sec," Charlotte said as Betty approached.

"Ladies, would either of you like another piece of cake? If so, you'd better grab it now before my husband and sons devour the rest."

Ella moaned, adamantly shaking her head. "Mrs. Love, as delicious as that cake is, I cannot fit another morsel of food inside this stuffed belly. But I will say that The Spicy Cajun Kitchen is my new addiction. They just might find me standing in line tomorrow. As for today, however, I am cutting myself off."

"Same for me," Charlotte chimed in.

"Well, we've got plenty of leftovers, so feel free to take some home if you'd like."

The moment Betty was out of earshot, Charlotte's smile faded. "What's the latest on the evidence that was collected at Manuel's crime scene? Did Lena get the results back yet?"

"She did. Nothing viable came of it."

"*None* of it?"

"Nope," Ella confirmed, her attention turning to Jake. Even from a distance, she could see the lines of distress etched in his expression. "Any DNA that could've come from Manuel's body or clothing was destroyed by the water. There were no fingerprints on the shell casings, and the serial numbers didn't match any of those stored in the network. The soil that was collected near Manuel's body contained remnants of his blood, but no one else's."

Charlotte stared out into the yard, taking a long sip of ginger beer. "You know, it's funny how life works. Here we were, thinking that the worst was behind us after the Numeric Serial Killer was locked up. We left River Valley behind and came to a new town to be with our significant others. I expected this fresh start to lead to some peace. But instead, we're right smack dab in the middle of another wild murder investigation."

Please don't say it, Ella thought, already knowing the direction her sister was taking the conversation.

"Since this case seems to be going left," Charlotte continued, "wouldn't now be a good time for you to tell Jake your big secret?"

"No," Ella whispered, her eyes darting from her sister to Jake. "It isn't. I already told you that I'll share it with him once the time is right. Now will you please drop it? *Especially* here?"

"Fine. But I'd be remiss if I didn't reiterate that the time was right when you first—"

"Will you *shush*!" Ella grabbed her arm, glad she'd only shared that she was seeing a therapist. Charlotte assumed it was to help her cope with the whole Numeric Serial Killer situation. She had no idea there was a way bigger secret being kept under wraps.

After the attack at the hospital, Ella thought she was ready to come clean and tell Charlotte the truth about what she'd been hiding. But then, she panicked. Ella wasn't prepared to deal with her sister's reaction, let alone the pressure she would've put on her to confess to Jake. He was at the height of the investigation. The news would ruin his focus, and in turn, wreck the case. The Love family, along with her own, had been through enough. Ella refused to be the cause of yet another devastating blow.

A pinch of her cheek pulled Ella from her thoughts.

"Look," Charlotte said right before Jake and Miles walked over. "I'll drop it. At least for now…"

Ella mouthed the words *thank you* just as Jake moved in, wrapping his arm around her waist.

"What are you two over here whispering about?"

"Probably the same thing you and your Clemmington PD cohorts were buzzing about over in the corner," Charlotte replied. "The Vincent Vineyard investigation."

"Yeah." Miles sighed. "Seems like that's all we're talking about these days." He brushed a few strands of hair away from Charlotte's eyes. "I haven't even had a chance to catch you up on all the latest."

"I think I'm up to date. Ella was just telling me about Manuel's autopsy results, and how nothing came of the DNA evidence collected at the crime scene."

Everyone turned to Jake, who was too busy checking his phone to notice the looks of concern on their faces.

"That's where we're at today," Miles said, giving his brother a reassuring shoulder bump. "But I have no doubt this case is about to take a turn in our favor."

"It sure is," Jake added, holding his cell in the air. "Especially now that Judge Pierce has finally signed the search warrant. Looks like we'll be paying Vincent Vineyard a visit first thing tomorrow morning."

The smile on Jake's face almost lifted Ella off her feet. It was the happiest she'd seen him in weeks.

"That is awesome, babe," she said, standing on her tippy toes and kissing his cheek. "I have a feeling this is gonna be it. Once you get inside those offices and start digging through the files, you'll find everything you need to make an arrest."

"Let's hope so. I certainly appreciate the vote of confidence." Jake raised his vodka tonic in the air. "You all know it wouldn't be right if I didn't make a toast."

"What are we toasting to?" Lena asked as she and David approached.

"Some sensational news," Miles told them while propping his beer bottle next to Jake's glass. "The warrant to search Vincent Vineyard has finally been signed!"

Lena and David responded with a resounding, "Yes!"

"Hey!" Kennedy called out from the sliding glass doorway. "You all better not be out here talking about you-know-what. Tonight is all about celebrating my wife. Remember, *none* of you are too old to be put in a time-out."

"Uh-oh," Jake uttered. "We'd better table this conversation for later."

Lena backed away, her right brow lifting slyly. "Fine. But don't think I'm not about to sneak over there and tell Dad about that search warrant."

"While you're at it," Miles interjected, "be sure to tell him that the renovations on the police station are finally done. You know, just so the conversation won't be *all* about the investigation."

"Good idea." Lena tapped her glass. "And afterward, who wants to grab another round?"

"I do!" Miles, Charlotte and David said in unison before following her toward the house.

Once they were alone, Jake tightened his grip on Ella's waist.

"Hey," he murmured, "have I mentioned lately how glad I am that you're here in Clemmington with me?"

"You haven't. But you can always mention it now if you'd like."

He placed a finger underneath her chin and lifted her head, their lips inches apart. "Ella Bowman, I am over the moon that you came all the way from River Valley, Nevada, to be here with me. And since I'm on the subject, have you given any more thought to moving here permanently?"

"I have."

"Oh, really? And?"

"*And*, I think I love that idea."

Jake squeezed her so tightly that she almost lost her breath. "Are you serious?"

"Yes. I'm serious!" she wheezed, laughing and choking at the same time.

Her moment of joy was interrupted by the sting of shame. Her secret loomed overhead like a violent storm cloud, as did the attacks and the threats—all of which she'd been keeping from the man she claimed to love.

Ella's smile shriveled. She knew there was only one way to fix the problem. And it didn't involve therapy, getting a job or running back to River Valley. It all came down to confessing the truth to Jake and finding the person behind the threats.

Chapter Sixteen

Jake banged on the door of Vincent Vineyard with a search warrant in hand and all of Clemmington PD in tow. Several moments passed. There was no response. He pounded the door once again.

"You're being too courteous," Miles said. "I say we kick that thing in and storm the place."

"I concur," Detective Campbell chimed in.

Jake jiggled the handle. The door opened. He turned to the officers and gave them a thumbs-up. "Let's go!"

The officers stormed the lobby, with Jake holding up his badge while taking a look around.

"Police!" he called out. "Clemmington PD is here to collect evidence as it pertains to the murders of Don Vincent and Manuel Ruiz. If you have any questions, you can meet us in the lobby and we'll be happy to address them."

Silence.

"Where the hell is everybody?" Miles asked.

"I have no idea. I'll do a quick search. See if I can find the family. In the meantime, let's stick to the plan. Lead the team upstairs and start inside the offices, removing any files, electronics, hard drives…anything that might contain pertinent information."

"Will do. If you need me, call me."

As Miles guided the officers upstairs, Jake heard a group of people cheering outside. He jogged toward the back of the lobby and peered out onto the deck. Claire, Tyler, Greer and their wives were standing at the bar in front of a crowd of people. They were each holding a bottle of wine in their hands as onlookers took photos.

Tyler stepped in front of the family and took a bow. "Thank you, everyone, thank you. Now, as you know, we consider all of you to be our Vincent Vineyard VIPs. You get premiere access to our newest offerings, and this group was the first to try the latest Cabernet Sauvignon. Today, I, along with the rest of the Vincent Vineyard staff, present to you that Cabernet's accompanying dessert wine." He turned toward the outdoor staircase and clapped his hands. "Servers!"

A group of staff members dressed in white shirts, burgundy vests and black slacks came rushing up the stairs, carrying trays filled with port glasses.

Jake observed the Vincents closely, watching

as Greer stood behind Tyler with a frown on his face. Jada and Faith were whispering frantically with one another while Claire stared out into the crowd in a complete daze. The investigation had clearly taken a toll on them. All except Tyler.

"Prepare your palates, my friends," Tyler continued, strolling through the rows of guests. "What you are about to experience is the perfect blend of warm dark chocolate and smooth ripe raspberries. Close your eyes. Imagine yourselves on a sexy getaway, lying next to your significant other. The mood is set. The energy is buzzing with passion. But instead of making love to your partner, you're sipping on this perfectly sweetened port."

"Oh, *please*," Greer moaned, gripping his stomach while leaning against the bar.

"It's tickling your taste buds," Tyler continued obliviously, "*exploding* inside of your mouth—"

"Mr. Vincent!" Jake interrupted, unable to bear another word.

The crowd turned in their seats, watching as the chief stepped onto the deck.

"Chief Love?" Tyler uttered. "What…what are you doing here? Can't you see I'm in the middle of a presentation? We're hosting an exclusive event for our most valued wine distribution companies. And I do not believe your name was on the guest list."

A few chuckles rippled through the crowd. But the majority of the guests appeared alarmed, as did Claire, Greer and Faith. Jada, however, marched over to Tyler and slipped her hand in his, as if to show her allegiance.

"Mr. Vincent, the reason why I'm here is because Clemmington PD has obtained a warrant to search the premises—"

"*Excuse* me?" Tyler interrupted right before Claire grabbed Greer's arm and yelled, "Go call our attorney! *Now*!"

Several guests turned their cell phones toward Jake and began filming.

"You're here to search the *premises*?" Tyler barked, storming over to Jake. "The hell you are. Let me see this warrant. And who signed it?"

"Judge Pierce," Jake replied coolly, handing him the document.

Greer shuffled over and snatched the paper out of Tyler's hand. "You cannot do this, Chief Love. What right do you have? What grounds are you even doing this on?"

"First of all, we're already doing it. My officers are inside your offices gathering evidence as we speak."

"They're *what*?" Claire screamed, attempting to run back inside before Faith held her back.

"Secondly," Jake continued, "Clemmington PD has reason to believe there is evidence here that's connected to the murders of Don Vincent and Manuel Ruiz. Third, and most importantly, please do not get in the way of my officers as they work to remove said evidence from the premises."

One of the guests recording the confrontation nudged the man sitting next to her, uttering, "Who knew we'd be getting a wine tasting *and* a show?"

"Okay, everyone," Jake said, waving his arms in the air. "The event is over. Please put your phones away and exit the premises. Mr. Vincent, could you show them a way out that doesn't require them to reenter the lobby?"

"You cannot do this," Tyler hissed.

"Chief Love," Claire cried, "could you at least wait until our attorney arrives before starting the search?"

"Too late, Mom," Greer told her, his phone stuck to the side of his face. "I'm still holding for the lawyer. Tyler, aren't you supposed to be showing our guests the way out?"

"I'm busy trying to put a halt to this…this *travesty*! And you should be helping me. Whose side are you even on?"

"The vineyard's, obviously. But this is not a good look! Now get these people the hell out of here!"

"Watch your mouth, little bro. Don't forget who's really running things around here."

"How could I? It's *me*!"

"*Hey*!" Jake interjected. "Just remove your guests from the premises, please. You'll have plenty of time to argue among yourselves once they're gone."

Ignoring their continued rumblings, Jake re-entered the building, sending one of his officers outside to monitor the evacuation while he headed upstairs to check on the search.

"Chief!" Miles called out.

Jake jetted toward the end of the hallway. "What's going on?"

"We've got a problem. Manuel's office has already been cleared out. And his computer is gone."

"*No*, come on! That's the main piece of equipment I was looking to seize. Let's make sure the team searches all the offices from top to bottom." Jake peered over the railing, staring down at the Vincents as they clamored inside the lobby. "While you all do that, I'll talk to the usual suspects. See if any of them know of its whereabouts."

As he rushed back down the stairs, there was a commotion near the front entrance.

"I said that Tyler Vincent is expecting me!" a

woman yelled before pushing her way past two officers.

Lauren Downs, host of a popular news and entertainment television show on WKMD-TV, came marching through the lobby with her camera crew in tow.

"Tyler!" she called out, flipping her bouncy platinum curls over her shoulder. "What in the hell is going on here? I could barely get inside! Why would you have law enforcement working the door and not tell them I'd be here filming a segment for my show? Did you forget that I'm covering the wine tasting event?"

For the first time, Jake saw Tyler lose his cool. He shooed his family members off to the side and ran over to Lauren, sweat visibly dripping down his face. "This way, guys!" he said to the production team.

"*Ew*," Lauren muttered after Tyler wrapped an arm around her. "Why are you perspiring like that?"

He ignored the question, panting uncontrollably while ushering her toward the deck.

"Excuse me," Jake said, "Ms. Downs, I'm sorry, but I'm going to have to ask you and your crew to leave. The vineyard is closed to the public at this time."

"*Public*," Lauren shot back. "I'm sorry, Chief Love, but are you aware of who I am? I am not the *public*. I am Clemmington, California's most watched, most influential television host—"

"I know exactly who you are, Ms. Downs. And this is in no way meant to offend you. But again, Vincent Vineyard is not open for business at this time. So I'm going to have to ask you to leave."

"*Chief*," Tyler sniffed, his eyes darting wildly. "Can you please just chill and let me take the crew out onto the deck for a few minutes so that I can speak with them in private?"

"I'm sorry, Mr. Vincent. But no. I cannot."

One of the men on Lauren's team whispered something in her ear. Her mouth fell open as she turned to Tyler, then Jake, then her cameraman. She threw him a hand signal. Within seconds, he began filming.

"Hello, ladies and gentleman," Lauren said into the camera. "I am reporting live from Vincent Vineyard."

"*Hey*!" Tyler yelled, lunging at the cameraman. "Cut that damn camera off!"

The man dodged Tyler's swipe and continued filming.

"We are here today to bring you breaking news."

Jake stepped in front of the camera. "Ms. Downs, please—"

"Vincent Vineyard has been overtaken by the

Clemmington Police Department," she interrupted, slowly moving toward the door while her crew followed, "as they continue to investigate the tragic murders involving the family."

Claire came running toward Lauren with her fists in the air. "Get out of my establishment before I—"

"Mom!" Greer yelled, holding her back while Tyler tried to knock the cameraman to the ground.

A couple of officers stepped in, subduing the Vincents while Jake moved the crew toward the exit.

"For the last time, Ms. Downs. I'm going to need for you to leave the premises. *Now.*"

"You heard the man!" Claire shrieked. "Get the hell out of here!"

The crew took their time, inching through the lobby. While the cameraman kept filming, Lauren kept reporting.

"As you can see, I am surrounded by complete and utter chaos. The entire Vincent family is in shambles over the deaths of Don Vincent and Manuel Ruiz. The scariest part of it all is that I may very well be standing in the midst of a cold-blooded killer! Chief Love," she continued, turning to him, "your father worked the Don Vincent murder investigation for *months* before throwing in the towel after he failed to solve it. You, a rookie police chief, recently reopened it. What makes you think you have what it takes to finally crack the case?"

She shoved the microphone in his face. Jake sucked in a sharp breath of air, his skin growing hot with irritation. "Didn't I tell you to—"

Watch it, he told himself. *You're on live television...*

"Ms. Downs, I will not be answering any questions regarding the investigation. Now this is the last time I'm going to ask you to leave. If you do not vacate the premises, I'll have no choice but to take you and your crew into custody."

"You witnessed that, ladies and gentlemen," Lauren said into the camera. "Chief Love has threatened to arrest my team and me as we attempt to report breaking news regarding the latest on the Clemmington serial killer." She shoved the microphone off to the side and leaned into Jake, whispering, "You haven't heard the last of me…"

Don't feed the trolls, he told himself, resisting the urge to kick the camera to the floor.

"Get out of here!" Claire screamed while charging the doorway. She stared out at the lawn, her eyes filling with tears as more reporters hurried up the walkway. "There's more of them! Where are they coming from?"

"Tyler called them here, Mom," Greer told

her. "Remember? We wanted to get the town excited about the new dessert wine. We had no idea the cops would show up with a search warrant."

"This is a disaster!" she cried into his shoulder. "And such an…an *embarrassment*. Vincent Vineyard will never recover from this."

Jake ran toward the reporters with his hands in the air. "Everyone, please. The event has been canceled and the vineyard is closed. We're going to have to ask you to leave the premises immediately."

"It doesn't look like it's closed," one of the reporters replied while continuing up the walkway. "What's going on here?"

"The police are raiding the place!" one of Lauren's crew members yelled. "They're looking for Don Vincent and Manuel Ruiz's killer!"

A chaotic scramble ensued as journalists bombarded Jake with questions.

"Chief Love! What new evidence did you find that brought you here today?" someone asked while another called out, "Chief! Who do you think committed the murders? Was it one of the Vincent family members? Are you prepared to make an arrest today?"

Jake marched to his car and popped open the truck, grabbing a roll of caution tape. Just as he headed back toward the building, law enforcement came filing out the door. Their hands were loaded with boxes and brown paper bags filled with evidence.

"*Horrible* timing," he mumbled, wincing as the reporters ambushed the officers. Jake ran back up the walkway and recruited Miles and Officer Underwood to help cordon off the area.

"Get back, please," Miles warned, blocking the microphones and cameras that journalists shoved in their faces. "Keep it up and I *will* take you to jail."

The warning sent reporters scurrying away from the entrance. But their cameras kept rolling, which meant the search and seizure would be all over the news.

"Well, I certainly didn't see this coming," Jake said to Miles. "Who knew today would turn into a damn media circus?"

"You never know. Maybe this is a good thing. All the attention might encourage someone to come forward with some information they've been sitting on."

"That's true. Between that and all this evidence we're collecting, something's got to come to the surface."

For the sake of this town and my reputation, it'd better...

Chapter Seventeen

Jake and Ella rode down Pacific Coast Highway, trailing behind Miles and Charlotte. They had just left a birthday celebration in Malibu thrown by an old high school friend of the Love brothers. Right before the festivities began to boil over, the foursome decided they'd better set off on the long drive back to Clemmington.

"Ooh," Ella groaned, slipping off her black suede booties. "I think I danced for about an hour too long in these shoes. Why didn't you tell me to sit down for a minute? Give my feet a break?"

"Because the DJ wouldn't stop playing all my favorite old school hip-hop songs, back-to-back. When the music's that good, there is no sitting down."

"*Facts*," Ella murmured as she dug her fist into the ball of her foot. "I may have fractured an ankle though. Nevertheless, I had a fantastic time."

She peered out the window, in awe of the rippling silver clouds drifting through the lavender-streaked sky. The sun was setting into the dazzling turquoise water. It brought on a fleeting sense of peace, as did the entire day. Good times were few and far between as the Vincent Vineyard murder investigation had taken over their lives.

Not only had Ella been fighting alongside Jake to help find the killer, but she'd been battling her own internal demons. The walls were closing in on her. Time was running out as the threats against her were intensifying. She'd be dead if it weren't for the construction worker thwarting the attack at the hospital. Next time, she might not be so lucky.

There shouldn't be a next time. You have got to tell Jake. Now.

"I love how everybody kept commenting on us being dressed alike," he said. "Little did they know we hadn't planned on wearing matching jeans, fitted T-shirts and leather jackets. It was a complete coincidence."

"Mmm-hmm…"

Jake gave Ella a nudge. "Why are you so quiet over there? Too much dancing? Champagne? Both?"

He let off a sexy chuckle—the kind that sent her straight inside the bedroom and in between the sheets. The day had been so perfect. She'd met his old high school crew, blushed when everyone called them the perfect couple and swooned when Jake professed how much he loved her. For the first time, she felt less like a girlfriend and more like a wife.

So why ruin all that now with your confession? Just enjoy the rest of the night. Go home and make love to your man. Save the admission for tomorrow...

"Hey," Jake said softly, reaching over and clutching her hand, "is everything all right?"

Ella turned to him. "Everything is perfect. I was just thinking about how amazing the day has been."

"I second that. And my favorite part of it, aside from you, of course, was *not* talking about the investigation. Today was all about fun, family, friends and us. We need more of this. Which means I have got to get this case solved so that I can focus on my woman and our future together."

When Jake tightened his grip on Ella's hand, the pressure almost squeezed the confession out of her. But she pursed her lips, allowing the tears that had welled in her eyes to trickle down her cheeks.

"Babe, what's wrong? Why are you crying? Did I say something to upset you?"

"No. Not at all. You said something, several things actually, that just warmed my heart."

And made me realize I probably don't deserve you.

"Good. That's what I like to hear. And if my words warmed your heart, just wait until you feel how my lips are gonna heat up that body of yours once we get home and I take off all your—"

Jake paused when his cell phone pinged through the speakers.

"Dammit! Just when I was getting to the good part." He jabbed the Accept button. "Chief Love."

"Chief!" someone screamed on the other end.

Ella jumped in her seat and checked the caller ID on the car's touch screen. It was Lucy, calling from the police station.

"I'm here," Jake said. "What's going on?"

"I just received a call from Claire Vincent. You need to get to the vineyard. Now!"

"Why? What happened?"

"Greer is dead!"

"Wh…what?" he stammered, pounding the phone's side button to increase the volume. "Greer is *what*?"

"He's dead!"

Ella covered her mouth right before a scream escaped her lips. She turned to Jake, whose arms were visibly shaking as he clutched the steering wheel.

"I'm on my way there now," Jake said before hanging up and scrolling the call log for Miles's name. The phone barely rang before he picked up.

"What's up, big bro? Did you and El change your minds and decide to come by for a nightcap and game of cards—"

"*Miles*. Listen to me. Greer is dead. Head to Vincent Vineyard. Now!"

JAKE PULLED INTO the vineyard's lot and threw the car into Park. He and Ella jumped out, gazing at the commotion swirling around them. Moments later, Miles and Charlotte arrived.

As the officers went running toward the crime scene, Charlotte grabbed hold of Ella.

"So let me get this straight. Greer's body was found inside the distillery?"

"Yes."

"Floating inside a vat of wine?"

"Yes. At least that's what Officer Underwood told Jake. He was the first one to arrive on the scene."

"*Oh, my God…*"

Law enforcement had blocked off the winery, only allowing a select few in and out. Tyler, who was standing off to the side of the entryway, struggled to keep his crumbling mother on her feet. Faith appeared completely inconsolable as her entire body shook within Jada's embrace.

"Who did this?" Faith screamed at Tyler over and over again. "Did you do this? I *know* you did this!"

He ignored her, focusing solely on his grief-stricken mother while Jada did her best to quiet Faith down.

Charlotte turned away from the family. "*Wow.* And you said that Claire was the one who found Greer's body?"

"Yes. Claire and her alleged lover, Alan Monroe."

"Ooh, that is terrible."

A weary sense of dread swarmed Ella's head. She opened the passenger door of Jake's car and slid down into the seat, begging her fatigued body not to give out on her—especially now that her mind had already begun to slip.

This is too much...

The chill of regret slithered across her skin. Ella should've confided in her sister a long time ago. Because then she could have divulged that after finding out Greer was dead, she'd received a text message saying, YOU'RE NEXT!

Ella jumped when someone tapped her shoulder.

"It's just me," Charlotte said softly. "Are you

okay? You're sitting here all hunched over, looking like you're about to pass out. Do you need some water? I think Miles has a case in the trunk."

"I *feel* like I'm about to pass out. But no. I'm fine."

Ella could feel Charlotte watching her intently. Knowing her sister, she saw right through her lie. Relief set in when Charlotte turned her attention back to the winery.

"It's weird that Alan Monroe is Vincent Vineyard's biggest competitor, yet he was here on the premises tonight. I mean, I get that he and Claire are involved or whatever, but what was he doing inside the distillery? Isn't that where their secret winemaking process takes place?"

"It is. Jake was wondering the same thing. Officer Underwood actually explained it all to him while we were on our way here. Which version of the story do you want? The long or the short?"

"The long version since it looks like we're gonna be here for a while."

"Okay, so, remember the day that Clemmington PD executed the search warrant here at the vineyard?" Ella asked.

"Yep, I do."

"Well, when law enforcement arrived, the Vincents were in the middle of hosting some exclusive tasting for a group of wine distributors. Claire wanted to invite Alan, but Tyler and Greer weren't having it. They thought it would be disrespectful to their father's memory—especially after she went behind their backs and invited Alan to that Cabernet Sauvignon tasting we attended. Plus, they were worried about him stealing their port wine idea and stocking it at his vineyard too."

With a wave of her hand, Charlotte dismissed the statement. "I bet Tyler and Greer were more concerned about Alan stealing the wine idea than they were their father's memory. But anyway, I digress. You may continue."

"Since Alan wasn't allowed to attend the event, Claire snuck him in today and was planning to do a private tasting for just the two of them after everyone went home. While she and Alan were attempting to pour the wine straight from the vat, nothing was coming out. They thought it was clogged. Alan climbed up to check and see what was going on. When he lifted the lid, there Greer was, lying inside."

"Already dead?"

Ella responded with a nod, unable to verbalize that yet another murder had been committed. She shuddered at the memory of lying on that cold hard hospital floor, almost being strangled to death. And that sharp object practically penetrating her skin inside the corn maze. Then the terrifying chase through the parking garage stairwell, the threatening text messages...

"Stop it!" she screamed, pressing her hand against her head, then jumping out of the car.

"El!" Charlotte ran after her. "What's wrong? Is talking about Greer's death too much for you to handle? If so, we can drop it."

"*All* of this is too much for me to handle! I messed up, Charlotte. Bad. *Real* bad."

"You messed up? What are you talking about?"

Ella released a trembling exhale, staring down at the ground while struggling to find the right words.

Just keep it simple. Start from the beginning.

She looked up at her sister. Ella's chest ached at the worry in Charlotte's eyes. "I'm so sorry."

"Sorry...sorry for what?"

"For what I've been hiding."

"Come on, El. Just spit it out. I'll never stop loving you no matter what it is. I bet you're just being dramatic and it isn't even that bad."

"Oh, but it is."

Charlotte grabbed hold of her. "*What* is?"

Say it. Just say it...

"I had an affair with Tyler," she finally blurted.

Hearing the words come out of her own mouth stopped time. Everything around Ella froze. Her vision blurred. She could no longer see Charlotte standing in front of her. But she could feel her sister's supportive grip slip from her shoulders.

"You did *what*?" Charlotte hissed.

"I had an affair with Tyler."

"Tyler *who*?"

Ella turned away, wishing the ground would part ways and swallow her up.

"Tyler Vin—*Vincent*," she sputtered as acid crept up her throat.

"*Ella*! How could you do something like that? When did this happen? *Why* did it happen? Oh, God…" Charlotte pressed her hands against her face, moaning into the night air. "I mean… *Tyler Vincent*? Of all people. Him? *Really*? You cannot be serious—"

"Will you please lower your voice?" Ella pushed Charlotte back inside the car and slammed the door, then climbed into the driver's seat. Her first thought was to start the engine and drive off. But she couldn't. She'd been running from the truth for long enough. It was time to face reality.

"Please tell me this is some sort of sick prank," Charlotte whispered.

"It's not. But I can explain."

"You'd better. Because *dammit*, Ella, this is not good. Especially now that the investigation has completely blown up."

Ella banged her head against the back of the

headrest, squeezing her eyes shut. "So, Tyler and I met several years ago at a wine festival in Reno. He wasn't married yet, but he and Jada were engaged. I had no idea though, because when he introduced himself, he told me he was single."

"Of course he did."

"Back then I really was single, plus I was traveling for work and just having a good time. When Tyler invited me to have a glass of wine with him, I did. That led to us taking a walk along The Row, then playing a few rounds of blackjack at his hotel casino. I wound up in his room for a nightcap, and…one thing led to another."

"Meaning?"

"Meaning we ended up sleeping together that night."

Charlotte inhaled sharply, glaring out the window while shaking her head. "I cannot believe what I'm hearing right now."

"Look, not to make excuses or anything, because I know this entire situation is an absolute mess."

"To put it lightly."

"But back when Tyler and I met, he wasn't nearly as arrogant and flashy as he is now."

"It's hard to imagine him being any other way."

Ella paused, swallowing the urge to address

her sister's snarky ad libs. "Anyway, Tyler and I ended up spending that entire weekend together. Once the festival was over, he came back to Clemmington, and I stayed in Reno. We did keep in touch and see one another whenever our schedules allowed. And what's interesting, even back then, Tyler talked about how badly he wanted to run Vincent Vineyard. I was always under the impression he'd stop at nothing to take over the top spot."

"Well, it looks like you were right. Because at this point, I'm thinking he's the one who's killing for it. But wait, how did you find out Tyler was engaged?"

"During a moment of eavesdropping here at the vineyard, ironically. A coworker had invited me to a charity event being thrown by Don to benefit underprivileged families. I was so impressed by his generosity that I had to support it. I decided not to tell Tyler I was coming and surprise him by just showing up. Little did I know *I'd* be the one getting the surprise after overhearing a guest discussing Tyler's engagement and elaborate wedding plans."

"Ugh," Charlotte groaned, clutching her chest. "What did he have to say for himself when you confronted him about it?"

"Nothing. Because I never got a chance to talk to him. I immediately stormed out of the event and left him a voice mail message stating that I knew the truth about everything. He never called back, and I never reached out again."

Dead air filled the car as both women sat silently, staring out the windshield.

You've got to tell her the rest...

"And, um…that's not all," Ella mumbled.

"There's *more*? What else could there possibly be?"

"I… I've been receiving threatening messages."

Charlotte reached over and gripped her hand. "What kind of threatening messages, Ella?"

"Texts, emails… It's someone telling me they know what I did and that I'd better get out of Clemmington. Tonight, after Greer's body was found, I received a message saying *you're next*."

"I cannot believe this! Why would you keep all of that from me? You didn't have to go through it alone, you know. I could've helped you. Hell, all of Clemmington PD could've helped you!"

"I know. But that would've meant having to tell Jake about Tyler and me. I just wasn't ready to face everything that would've come along with that."

"Is there anything else I should know?"

"Yes," Ella whispered, staring down at her trembling hands. "That attack at the corn maze? It wasn't the only one. I was chased through

Gateway Park after one of our workouts at the track, and assaulted inside the hospital that day you took me to the job interview—"

"*See*," Charlotte interrupted, throwing her hands in the air, "I knew something was wrong that day at the hospital when you got back inside the car! Digital threats are one thing. But physical attacks that you kept to yourself instead of reporting? Not even to me? El! What were you thinking?"

"What was I thinking? I was thinking about Jake, and how he'd just been promoted to chief. I didn't wanna ruin his focus and taint our relationship with news that I'd dated one of his main suspects. I was also thinking about you, and Miles, and everything you'd been through trying to catch the Numeric Serial Killer."

"As if you didn't go through hell right along with us. You're lucky you weren't killed."

Charlotte's grasp on Ella's hand tightened. Through it, Ella could feel the love. She could also see the devastation in her sister's watery red eyes. The sight triggered an unbearable sense of guilt.

"I'm just glad you're okay," Charlotte insisted. "And I will see to it that you stay that way. Now, my guess is that Tyler's behind the attacks. He may fear you're going to ruin his reputation by blasting the news that he's an unfaithful pig to the entire town. He'd be so embarrassed. Also, you're dating the chief of police, whose number one priority is solving this case. If something happened to you, it could throw Jake off and botch the investigation. See where I'm going with all this?"

"I do."

"Oh, and speaking of the chief of police, when are you going to tell him—"

Ella waved her hand in the air. "Please don't start with that line of questioning. I am planning to tell Jake everything."

"When?"

"When the time is right."

A knock on the glass sent both women jolting in their seats.

"Jake!" Ella shrieked, rolling down the window. "You scared us!"

"Sorry, babe. Listen, it looks like we're gonna be a while. I don't want to leave you two in the parking lot waiting for us. El, why don't you go back to Charlotte's place and wait for me there? I'll pick you up as soon as we're done."

She nodded, studying the creases lining his face. The pained expression was a far cry from the look of elation he'd worn as they were heading back from Malibu, before getting Lucy's call.

And now you're about to twist the knife in his heart by admitting to the affair with Tyler...

"How's it going in there?" Charlotte asked.

"It's bad. Really bad. The medical examiner is processing Greer's body now. He's got a bullet wound to the right temple. Lena found a couple of twenty-two caliber shell casings—the same kind that were at Manuel's crime scene—underneath one of the wine racks. And let me say this. While I've got my eyes on everybody, I am having a hard time figuring out who might be behind this. The entire family is distraught. Even Tyler, in his own weird way."

"Chief!" one of the officers called out.

"I'll be right there!" Jake shouted over his shoulder.

"We'd better let you get back to work," Ella told him.

"You two be careful. El, text me as soon as you all make it in and let me know you're safe."

"*Tuh,*" Charlotte uttered, patting her purse. "Don't worry. According to my Glock twenty-two, we'll be just fine."

"I know you will." Jake turned to Ella. "Love you."

"Love you too," she muttered, her lips stinging with remorse as he kissed them softly.

Her eyes glazed over as she watched Jake hurry back inside the distillery.

"Come on," Charlotte said quietly. "Let's get you out of here."

Ella started the engine and pulled out of the lot in a daze, contemplating how in the hell she'd get up the nerve to tell Jake the truth.

Chapter Eighteen

The Daily Herald

OPINION

*Clemmington's Police Department is failing
the community.
It may be time to send in the Feds...*

By Lauren Downs

Ms. Downs is a news and entertainment reporter for WKMD-TV and a former criminal justice professor at Valley Oak Community College.

CLEMMINGTON—I recently received a personal invitation to attend a wine tasting event at Vincent Vineyard in celebration of their newly released tawny port. With my production crew in tow, I set off on what was promised to be an amazing experience filled with exclusive guests, a private tour and, of course, great wine.

Needless to say, it wasn't.

Before arriving at the vineyard, I spoke with Tyler Vincent, who at the time was serving as co-vice president of Vincent Vineyard along with his brother, Greer Vincent. We discussed conducting an interview that would air on WKMD-TV, announcing the winery's new dessert wine, exciting plans for the future and more. When I got there, however, our plans took a sharp turn.

I was not greeted by the Vincents. Instead, I was bombarded by the Clemmington Police Department—Chief Jake Love to be exact. He informed me that the vineyard was closed to public access and asked my crew and I to leave without telling us why. I was confused by the request, considering there was a large group of guests bustling about on the back deck.

Then suddenly, chaos ensued. Law enforcement officers came marching out of the business offices carrying electronics, cardboard boxes and brown paper bags. My producer was the first to realize that the vineyard was being raided, which is understandable, considering the recent murder of Manuel Ruiz, Vincent Vineyard's longtime manager, and now Greer Vincent. Connecting the killings to the business is a no-brainer, especially after the owner, Don Vincent, was found stabbed to death in the vineyard's grape fields around this time last year.

Here's where things get interesting. Claire Vincent was set to name one of her sons president of Vincent Vineyard in the coming days. It is no secret that the brothers had been at odds since their father's death, both vying for the top spot. Ironically, Greer Vincent turned up dead right before the announcement. Days later, a press release landed in my email inbox stating that Tyler Vincent had been named president. Instead of humbly (and quietly) accepting the promotion while mourning his brother's death, Tyler and his wife, Jada Vincent, threw an extravagant party in celebration of the appointment. Is it just me, or can anyone else smell the suspicion surrounding such narcissistic behavior?

For most of us, the writing is on the wall. Clemmington PD, however, is turning a blind eye to the truth. While the Love family has somehow managed to attract their fair share of serial killers (from Lena

Love's Heart-Shaped Murder investigation to Miles Love's Numeric Serial Killer case), they did apprehend those criminals within a reasonable amount of time. The Vincent Vineyard Assassin, however, continues to elude police more than a year later. Who will be next? Will the murders spread beyond the vineyard and spill over into the Clemmington community? Is our police department capable of preventing that from happening? Unfortunately, my guess is no.

I understand that Chief Love is new to his position and has something to prove. But there comes a time when a man must admit that he is in over his head. Don Vincent's murder occurred during retired Chief Kennedy Love's tenure, who served on the force for over thirty-five years. If he could not solve the case, I highly doubt that Chief Jake Love, who just so happens to be the former chief's son, can.

How can Clemmington PD get justice for these victims, their families and our entire community? The answer is simple: send in the Feds.

Chapter Nineteen

"Thank you so much!" Ella said as she exited Nancy's Country Mart.

Nancy raised her hand feebly, barely looking Ella's way while waving goodbye.

The tone of the town had changed since Lauren Downs's op-ed in *The Daily Herald* hit newsstands. There was a clear divide between the community and the police department, and the Love family in particular could feel the public's disdain.

Jake continued to stand his ground in the midst of it all, refusing to call on the Federal Bureau of Investigation for assistance.

"Clemmington PD does not need help from the Feds," he'd say whenever the topic came up during press conferences. "I believe in this agency. We are perfectly capable of solving this case on our own. We've got three people on the force who helped bring down two prolific serial killers. My officers will utilize those same skills to solve this investigation."

In the meantime, Ella had been doing all that she could to keep Jake's spirits up while struggling through her own private battles. She had yet to tell him about the affair with Tyler, despite swearing to Charlotte that she would.

"Stop making false promises and tell him before it's too late!" Charlotte kept insisting.

"I will!" Ella would always reply. "I'm just waiting for the right time."

What she hadn't realized was that there never would be a right time. Confessing the affair was going to be difficult no matter the moment, place or mood.

Telling Jake tonight was out of the question. Ella had already decided to make it an upbeat evening. He needed it. She'd even nixed their healthy eating agenda and picked up one of Nancy's gourmet meat lover's pizzas and a bottle of Pinot Grigio.

Balancing the pizza box and bottle in one hand and alarm fob in the other, she hurried across the dim parking lot. Her electric-blue Jeep came into view. She clicked the button and reached for the door handle.

"*Ouch!*" she shrieked when a sharp edge of chipped paint sliced her skin.

Ella shook her hand, hoping the cool air would

soothe the sting. She took a step back and studied the door. Long jagged white lines had been carved into the paint.

"Now I know my car didn't get keyed…" she griped, opening the door and dumping everything inside. She pulled out her cell phone and tapped on the flashlight, shining it along the surface. The scratches ran from the front to the back doors and all around the perimeter.

She hesitated at the sight of a red mass sticking out from underneath the vehicle. "What in the…"

Fear tore through Ella's limbs as slid her trembling hand underneath the car and poked at the mass. It felt like a lump of satiny material. Pinching it between her index finger and thumb, she gradually pulled the material. Relief hit when she realized it was just a silk scarf.

Holding it up to the phone's light, Ella wondering how the designer piece had landed underneath her car. She figured it had slipped from someone's neck and headed back toward the store to turn it in.

Her fingers skimmed a clump of thick raised stitching. She paused underneath a light pole. A set of initials were embroidered on one end of the scarf.

"JV," Ella read aloud as she continued toward the entrance.

She stopped, staring back down at the initials. "JV, JV…"

Her entire body went numb.

Jada Vincent.

A thousand thoughts flashed through her mind—one being more prevalent than all the rest. Jada was the killer.

It was time to talk to Jake. About everything.

"THIS IS DELICIOUS, EL," Jake said, reaching for a third slice of pizza. "Meat lovers was a great idea. Not to mention a nice break from all the salads."

Ella stared at him from across the dining room table. Shifting in her seat, she whispered, "Hey, there's, um… There's something I need to tell you."

He popped a piece of pepperoni inside his mouth. "Hmm. You know what else was a great idea? Dropping all talk of the investigation. At least for tonight."

"Jake? Did you hear me?"

"Hear what?"

"I said I need to tell you something."

"Oh, no. Sorry, babe. I was too busy blabbering about Nancy's amazing pizza. Go on. I'm listening."

Just say it…

"Remember that day you took me to Vincent Vineyard for the wine tasting?"

"Yeah. Why?"

"It, um… It wasn't the first time I'd been there."

Jake's eyelids lowered, his head tilting in confusion. "What do you mean?"

Ella slid her plate to the side, the sight of food causing a sudden bout of nausea. "I'd visited the vineyard once before. A few years ago, after being invited by someone in the family."

"Hold on," Jake said, dropping his slice of pizza. "One of the Vincents invited you to the vineyard? You never mentioned knowing any of them. Who was it?"

Ella dug her fingernails into her thighs so deeply that she almost drew blood.

Rip the bandage off and tell him!

"It was Tyler."

"*Tyler.* But…why? *How?* You two don't even know one another."

Remaining silent, Ella's gaze fell from Jake's twisted expression down to her plate.

"What am I missing here?" he pressed.

This is it. You've ruined everything…

She looked up and blurted, "Tyler and I had an affair."

Jake's head swiveled, his ear thrust in her direction. "I'm sorry. I think I must've misheard you. You and Tyler *what*?"

"He and I had an affair. And before you say anything, please know that I would've told you sooner, but I didn't want to throw you off the investigation. Not to mention jeopardize our relationship."

Jake pushed away from the table, his glare filled with venom. "You had an affair with Tyler Vincent, and didn't think it was a good idea to tell me?"

His eerily low tone sent a chill straight through Ella.

"Yes," she whispered. "But he wasn't married yet. I had no idea he was even engaged. And I was going to tell you eventually. I just couldn't seem to find the right time."

"I cannot believe this. It…it doesn't even make sense. Are you still in contact with him?"

"No! Of course not."

Jake stood so abruptly that his chair flipped over. "I'm sorry. I cannot do this," he scoffed, rushing out of the room. Ella reached for him as he flew by. He jerked away and stormed toward the bedroom.

"See?" she yelled. "This is exactly why I didn't want to tell you!"

Bam!

Ella winced when the bedroom door slammed behind him.

"You know what?" she cried out. "I can't do this either!"

She snatched her keys and cell phone off the kitchen counter and ran out the door. Tears blurred her vision as she tore down the stairs and onto the street. Ella turned right, then left, then ran in the direction of Charlotte's house.

The cool night air chilled her skin. Light rain drizzled from the sky while dense fog rolled from dark gray clouds. A jacket would've done her some good. But staying warm was the last thing on Ella's mind.

My worst nightmare is now my reality. Jake and I are over...

A sharp rock dug into the sole of her shoe. She'd left the loft so fast that she hadn't changed out of her UGG slippers. Ella ignored the pain and sped up as sobs ripped through her chest.

Headlights blinked behind her. She spun around, her hair whipping across her face. Jake's dark sedan appeared in the distance. Ella bent down, propping her hands on her knees while heaving uncontrollably. Between the sprints and the stress, she was practically hyperventilating.

It's okay. He came for me...

The sedan slowed down, then pulled to the curb. She waved, tears of relief streaming down her face.

"I'm sorry, Jake!" Ella yelled when the car

door opened. "I shouldn't have left like that. I should have stayed back so we could talk. But I'm so glad you came…"

Her voice trailed off when someone stepped out. The silhouette was hard to see through the darkness. But it didn't appear to be Jake.

Ella stood straight up and peered at the car. The headlights had been turned off. She couldn't decipher the license plate.

"Jake? Is that… Is that you?"

The figure remained silent while continuing to approach.

Oh, no. Oh, no… Run!

Just as Ella began backing away, the figure came charging toward her.

"*Ahh!*" she screamed before being knocked to the ground. "Stop! Get off of me!"

Ella clawed at the attacker's face, struggled to remove the black ski mask. Shreds of wool snagged her fingernails.

"Take off that mask! Show your face, you coward!"

Pow!

Blood filled Ella's mouth as a punch to her jaw cut against her teeth. She swung her fist in the air and cracked what she hoped was the assailant's nose. Judging by the guttural scream, she had.

Ella drew back her leg and kicked as hard as she could. The attacker fell back against a tree trunk, groaning, then sliding to the ground. Ella scrambled to her feet and lunged at him, struggling to pull off the ski mask.

"I was ready for you today!" she yelled. "Come on, bitch. Show your face! Is that you, Tyler?"

The killer jumped up and lunged at Ella. This time, she caught a glimpse of a silver blade shining underneath a streetlight.

"*Nooo*!" she screamed, ducking to her left, then charging toward the middle of the street. He chased after her, playing a game of cat and mouse as they dodged in between cars.

"Somebody help me!" Ella screamed. She ran toward the corner, realizing she was only a block away from Charlotte's house.

Make a run for it. GO!

The fog turned her around. Was her house to the right? Or the left?

"You gotta be quicker than that," the attacker growled before lunging at Ella once again.

Her body slammed against the edge of the curb. Ella tried to scream out in pain. But her cries were muffled by the assaulter's gloved hand.

He grabbed the sides of her head, twisting in an attempt to snap her neck. Ella stiffened her muscles and pressed her thumbs into the attacker's eyes.

"You *bitch*!" he hollered, grabbing hold of her face.

Ella rammed her elbow against his temple then

jumped to her feet. Just as she jetted forward, he kicked her legs out from underneath her.

"And now you're going to die!" he hissed.

The attacker jumped on top of her, his knees pinned against her arms. He covered her mouth with one hand and gripped her neck with the other.

She gasped for air, willing herself to get up again. Fight back. To no avail.

The veins in her head tightened. Pressure in her throat mounted as the air grew thin. Her chest heaved, her body struggling for oxygen.

This is it. This time, I really am going to die...

A car engine roared in the distance. Lights blinked while a horn blew. Ella felt her cell phone vibrating against her hip. She struggled to reach for it just as a blade grazed her cheek.

"Touch that phone and I will slice open your throat!"

The car looming in the distance moved in closer. Its siren blared.

The assailant flinched, momentarily letting up on his grip.

"Help me!" Ella was finally able to scream. "*Please!*"

The car jumped the curb and came to an abrupt halt. Someone jumped out. Heavy footsteps pounded the asphalt.

The attacker attempted to hop up and escape.

"Oh, no you don't," Ella gasped. She grabbed his ankle and pulled him to the ground. He responded with a kick to her head.

"*Dammit!*" she screamed as he ran toward Gateway Park's entrance.

"Freeze! Drop the knife and put your hands in the air!"

Jake!

Ella rolled over onto her knees and attempted to stand. "*Go*," she choked, directing Jake toward the park. "Get him!"

Jake ran after the assailant as he tried to kick open the gate. It was locked. Just when he began climbing it, Jake grabbed the attacker by his hoodie and pulled him to the ground.

"Drop your weapon!" he yelled with his gun drawn. "It's over. You're done!"

The attacker tossed the knife toward Jake's feet. A rush of adrenaline shot through Ella at the sight of surrender. She rushed over as Jake pulled the suspect to his feet and handcuffed him.

"And now," Jake said, "the moment of truth. We finally get to see who's been terrorizing this town for over a year."

He pulled off the assailant's mask. Shined his flashlight in the killer's face.

Jake and Ella gasped in unison.

It was Faith.

Chapter Twenty

"Thank you, Dr. Allison," Jake said into the phone. "I appreciate you letting me know Ella made it to the hospital. Yes, please call back and let me know how she's doing once you're done with the examination."

He disconnected the call and rushed back toward the interrogation room, where Miles was questioning Faith. On the way there, Jake was stopped by Officer Underwood.

"Chief, Ben Foray just walked into the station and gave us an official statement."

"Oh, really. What does he have to say for himself?"

"Well, after he heard that Faith was arrested—"

"Wait, he already knows about that?" Jake interrupted. "Damn, news travels fast in this town."

"It does. But he wanted to state on the record that he had nothing to do with any of the murders. He did admit to knowing Faith, and said they met when he was performing community service at the school where she was taking computer classes. When she found out he was into fraudulent activities, she hired him to take that tour of Vincent Vineyard and steal the paperwork from Don's office."

"But she works there. Why didn't she just take it herself?"

"Because she didn't want to get caught on camera. She thought Ben could get away with grabbing the documents, and if he got caught during the process, he could pull the whole I-got-lost-during-the-tour stunt. That didn't work, obviously."

The sound of Faith's shrill ranting echoed through the hallway.

"I'd better get back to this interrogation," Jake said, slowly backing away. "Do not let Ben leave here before I speak with him."

"I won't. Oh, and one more thing. You know that amendment to Don Vincent's will that Ben stole? He brought it in with him. Said that Faith wanted him to alter it so that instead of the vineyard being left to Greer, it would be left to Tyler."

Jake stopped abruptly. "But wait…why would Faith want Vincent Vineyard to be left to Tyler instead of her own husband? You must have gotten their names mixed up."

"That's what I'd thought initially too. But I didn't. I'm repeating Ben's exact words. I actually had him run it by me three times. You can verify his statement once you're done questioning Faith."

"Yeah, I will. Because that's weird…"

Jake entered the interrogation room. Faith sat silently across from Miles, the wild grin on her face appearing as though she were in the front row of a comedy club rather than a police station.

"Mrs. Vincent," Miles began, "why don't you share with Chief Love what you just told me?"

She turned in her seat, batting her sparse eyelashes at Jake. "What, that I've been having an affair with Tyler Vincent?"

Instead of seating himself coolly, Jake practically fell into his chair. "I'm sorry. Could you please repeat that?"

She leaned in closer, yelling, "I've been having an affair with Tyler Vincent!"

The room went silent. Jake remained motionless, knowing that if he didn't react, Faith would keep talking.

"I know, I know," she continued, waving her cuffed hands in the air. "I seem too *sweet* and… and *demure* to be with a man so flamboyant, right? It is idiotic, if we're being totally honest here. But that was okay. Because somehow, it worked. You see, I had enough brains for us both. And he had the showstopping presence to represent Vincent Vineyard. Take it to a level far beyond its competitors."

Jake grabbed a bottle of water, his hand shaking as he took several long swallows. He'd seen a lot during his time on the force. But nothing like this.

"You know," the chief began after composing himself, "you're a great actress, Mrs. Vincent. I never would've suspected you were the one behind all this chaos. How long have you and Tyler been seeing one another?"

"Several years," she murmured, her smirk shriveling into a tight scowl. "Believe you me, I hadn't planned on being a mistress for that long. But Tyler tends to make promises that he has a hard time keeping. So, I had to start making moves that would incentivize him to leave his wife."

Miles frantically scribbled down her words, only pausing to ask, "Incentivize, meaning to commit murder?"

"Very good, Detective Love! See, you get me." Faith slid down in her chair, her eyes fixated on the back wall. "Tyler had me doing things I never thought I would. But the goal was to get rid of anything standing in the way of him taking over the vineyard, and us being together. So, I did what I had to do in order to make that happen."

"But why kill your husband?" Jake asked. "The idea of getting a divorce never crossed your mind?"

Faith rolled her eyes. "Murder is clean, Chief Love. In death, you're just...*poof*! Gone. Done. There's no fuss. No splitting things up. No talk of, *no, I get the house*! Or, *you can't have that car*! Divorce is messy. And lingering. Not to mention frowned upon within the Vincent family. Had I left Greer, I would have been ostracized and out of a job. Because who knows when Tyler would've actually left Jada? Plus, everyone sympathizes with a widow. Not a divorcée."

"Damn," Miles muttered. "That's cold. So how did you manage to get Greer's body inside of that wine vat? Did you have help?"

"*Help*? Of course not. I'm not stupid, Detective Love. I work alone. Nothing is a secret if someone else knows about it. I got Greer inside the vat by convincing him that the spout was faulty. Asked him to climb up and take a look, see what may have jammed it. When he did, I shot him in the head. He fell forward, I pushed him all the way in, dropped the lid and that was it."

Despite the heat blowing through the vent, a chill fell over the room. Jake had heard enough. He was burning to throw her in jail. But there was more work that needed to be done.

"Hey, don't look so somber, you two!" Faith quipped. "At least Greer died surrounded by what he loved most. *Wine.* But anyway, back to the reason I did all of this in the first place. Claire was on the verge of naming Greer president of the vineyard. And I couldn't let that happen. He was weak, and way too humble. You all saw him on stage that night at the casino. He was a bumbling embarrassment. Knowing that was my husband, getting upstaged by the man *I* should've been there with, was infuriating. That should have been *me* out there strutting up to the stage, hand in hand with Tyler while singing 'Welcome to the Jungle,' not Jada!"

"Since you mentioned Jada," Jake interjected, "tell me, did she know Ben Foray?"

"No. Well, not until her nosy ass walked in on me talking to him about breaking into Don's office the day of the tour. Once I realized she'd overheard me, I tried to get her in on it, especially since it was her husband's name being forged onto the amendment. But she refused. However, I did swear her to secrecy, and she stuck to her word."

"And she didn't question why you'd want Tyler

to take over as president instead of your own husband?"

"Of course not. Jada may be a fool, but she was wise enough to know that a dry, dull man like Greer could not have handled that position. Plus, she had no idea Tyler was leaving her for me."

Probably because he wasn't, Jake wanted to say. But he refrained.

When Faith's voice cracked, he thought she was on the verge of bursting into tears. Instead, she broke into a fit of giggles.

"Wanna hear a fun little fact?" she asked. "When I first met Ben, I had him save my number in his phone under Jada's name. You know, as a precaution, just in case the wrong eyes happened to see me calling."

Jake threw Miles a knowing glance. He nodded, understanding that it had been Faith calling Ben that night at the Hole in the Wall, not Jada.

"It really is unfortunate that you chose to take the lives of Don, Manuel and Greer over greed and lust, Mrs. Vincent," Jake said. "I'm just glad we caught you when we did. Had we not, Ella Bowman would probably be dead, and I have no doubt that Jada would've been next."

He paused, waiting for her to respond. She didn't.

"Did you plant Jada's scarf underneath Ella's car at Nancy's Country Mart?"

Faith stared down at her wrists, running her fingertip along the edge of the cuffs. "Yep. I had to pin the crimes on somebody, didn't I? Look, don't feel bad for Jada. She is not a victim. She's a rotten bully. She doesn't deserve her title as director of *anything*, let alone the honor of being Tyler's wife. With her in prison and everyone else out of the way, Tyler would be president of Vincent Vineyard, we'd get married and live out our happily-ever-after."

Jake recoiled at the flat, cavalier tone in her voice. She spoke as if she were reading through a grocery list rather than confessing to her horrific crimes.

"Why kill Manuel though?" he asked. "He wasn't even in the running to taking over the vineyard."

"But he *was* planning on speaking with law enforcement, now wasn't he? In case you haven't figured this out, Chief Love, I didn't just use those newfound computer skills to design Vincent Vineyard's website. I also used them to hack into Manuel's computer after I saw him chitchatting with law enforcement during the Cabernet Sauvignon tasting, then at the casino event. I knew he was up to something. And I was right. Manuel had secretly audited the vineyard's financial records and *allegedly* found proof that Tyler had been embezzling money."

"Oh, did he?" Jake grabbed his cell phone and sent Detective Campbell a message, requesting that he bring Tyler in for questioning. "So is it safe to assume that you killed Manuel before he could reveal what he'd learned about Tyler?"

A condescending chuckle gurgled in the back of Faith's throat. "Umm, *yeah*. What else was I supposed to do? Sit back and let you find all that evidence, then watch my man go to jail? That would've totally ruined our plans for the future. Manuel left me no choice but to kill him."

As Faith's pupils began to dilate, Jake contemplated placing her on a 5150 hold.

"Plus," she muttered, her head pivoting away from the officers, "Manuel knew about my affair with Tyler."

"How did he find out about it?" Miles asked.

"He caught us making out one night inside the distillery."

"Did Tyler know anything about these murders and the other crimes you were committing?"

"No! He did not. So don't even try and drag him into this. That man is innocent. Leave him alone so he can help assemble my defense team and get me the hell out of here. Speaking of which, when can I post bond?"

"*Bond*?" Jake shot back. "Mrs. Vincent, you murdered three people and attempted to murder a fourth. There will be no bond."

Faith's expression fell into a rumpled frown. Jake thought he'd finally humbled her into facing the ramifications of her actions. But then she stretched out, crossing her legs and looking up at him with a sinister gleam in her eyes. The devilish scowl was unlike anything he'd ever seen.

"I know my actions may be vile," she admitted. "But guess what? It feels good to finally be seen. And heard. And feared. Do you know how hard it is to constantly stand in the background? In the shadows of my inadequate husband, and that disco queen freak show, Jada? I could run that vineyard by myself better than any of the Vincents. But I don't have the looks. Or all that fake ass razzle-dazzle. I'm about the business. Which, unfortunately, doesn't bode well within a sea of superficiality."

Jake's head tilted as he studied Faith's smug demeanor. "Mrs. Vincent, did it ever occur to you that Tyler was just using you for your business acumen? Because I certainly haven't seen any proof that he and Jada were in the process of divorcing. Have you, Detective Love?"

"Nope. Not a shred."

The spark in Faith's fiery gaze dimmed. That curve in her lips straightened as she pulled her feet back underneath the chair. "But I... I know he was working toward it. Privately, I'm guessing..."

"Let's talk about Ella Bowman," Jake said.

"What about her?"

"Why were you targeting her with the threats and attacks?"

"Because of her affair with Tyler."

The words stung like acid seeping through Jake's eardrums. They burned just as badly as they had when Ella first shared the news.

He turned away from Faith, unable to bear her sneering grin.

"*Aww*," she whimpered. "Did hearing that upset you, Jake? I'm so sorry. If I weren't handcuffed, I'd reach out and give you a hug—"

"That's enough," Miles interrupted. "And it's Chief Love to you. Now let's stay on course here. What was your motive behind the attacks on Ella?"

"It's simple. I was jealous. Once I overheard Tyler telling Greer he was worried about her being here in Clemmington and putting their affair on blast, that was it. I knew I had to get rid of her. And before you even say it, I don't care *when* the affair took place. It happened. Plus, how was I to know whether or not Ella came to Clemmington to try and woo Tyler away from me? I wasn't taking any chances. Period."

"Well, how were you able to track her every

move?" Jake asked. "Did you hack into her email as well?"

"*Maybe*," Faith purred coyly. "That, and I *could've* placed a GPS tracker on her Jeep as well…"

Leaning back in his chair, Jake crossed his arms over his chest. "Welp, now you'll get to spend the rest of your life in prison over a man who cared nothing about you."

"Without the possibility of parole, I'm sure," Miles chimed in.

"Not only that," Jake continued, "but the woman you and Tyler were hurting the most? Jada? I bet she'll be named president of Vincent Vineyard. Mark my words. Faith Vincent, you are under arrest for the murders of Don Vincent, Manuel Ruiz and Greer Vincent, and the attempted murder of Ella Bowman. Officer Underwood is on his way in to book you." The chief stood, sauntering toward the door. "Oh, and one more thing. Thanks for the tip on Tyler's embezzlement. He'll be facing a hefty fine and three years in prison."

"He'll be facing *what*?" Faith screamed. "No! You can't do that. I didn't even mention anything about Tyler embezzling money. Or did I? If I did, I take it back. And if you didn't record it, I didn't say it!"

"Oh, but I did record it," Miles said, waving his

cell phone in the air. "And once we recover Manuel's missing laptop, which I'm sure we'll find at your house, that'll confirm your admission."

"You can't search my house! Where's your warrant?"

"I'll be filing an emergency request to have one issued momentarily," Jake told her before walking out, signaling Officer Underwood over, then calling the hospital to check on Ella.

Chapter Twenty-One

Ella turned off the television and kissed Jake's forehead as he dozed on the couch.

"I knew you wouldn't be able to make it through the entire movie," she murmured.

"What do you mean?" Jake asked, popping up and blinking rapidly. "I wasn't asleep!"

She burst out laughing and stood, pulling him to his feet. "Liar. Come on. Let's go to bed."

"You don't have to tell me twice." He leaned in and kissed her neck on the way to the bedroom. "Plus, I know you've gotta get some rest for your big day tomorrow."

"Yes, I do. Clemmington General Hospital's neonatal unit is expecting me bright and early."

"My girl. I'm so proud of you. Nurse Bowman, reporting for duty!"

Before she entered the room, Jake slipped her hand in his, stopping her in the doorway.

"Listen," he said softly, "I know we agreed to bury certain topics when it comes to the Vincent

Vineyard investigation. But I just want to reiterate how happy I am that you've been in therapy, and apologize again for the way I reacted when you told me about you and Tyler's—"

Ella held her finger to his lips. "You don't have to do that. You've already apologized, and I've accepted it. I understood your reaction. I expected it, really, especially after the way I mishandled the entire situation."

"But I just… I can't help but blame myself for you being attacked that night after I stormed off and you left the house."

"That attack led us to the killer. Getting there may have been brutal, but we did it. And now, you're the hero for finally solving one of Clemmington's biggest cases."

"It never would've happened without your help," Jake whispered, kissing her gently before heading inside the room.

"We do have our cell phone location trackers to thank too," Ella said while turning down the bed. "Thank goodness you were smart enough to suggest we turn them on, and you thought to come after me—" She stopped abruptly when her hand hit what felt like a rock.

"*Ouch*! What was that?"

Jake walked up behind her, wrapping his hands around her waist. "I don't know. Why don't you reach underneath your pillow and find out?"

"Mr. Love, what are you up to?" Ella flipped her pillow over. There, lying on the mattress, was a small red velvet box.

She gasped, her body falling back against his. "Is that what I think is?"

"There's only one way to find out."

Tears sprang to Ella's eyes as she reached for the box. She slowly opened it. A yellow peanut M&M sat in the middle.

"*Jake*!" she screeched, spinning around and banging her hands against his chest. "Why would you trick me like that and—"

The sight of an emerald cut diamond engagement ring propped between his fingertips silenced her.

Jake dropped down on one knee.

"Ella Bowman," he said, taking her hand in his, "once you're done enjoying that peanut M&M, would you do me the honor of being my wife?"

"Yes. *Yes*! Of course!"

The moment Jake slipped the ring on her finger, Ella pulled him to his feet and jumped in his arms.

"Never have I ever thought I'd be this happy," she whispered into his chest.

"Never have I ever thought I'd find a woman like you. Thank you."

"Thank me? For what?"

"For renewing my faith in love."

* * * * *